CRY WOLF

CRY WOLF SERIES BOOK 1

KAREN FULLER

This is a work of fiction. Names, characters, places, and incidents are products of the author's imagination or are used fictitiously and are not to be construed as real. Any resemblance to actual events, locations, organizations, or persons, living or dead, is entirely coincidental.

World Castle Publishing, LLC

Pensacola, Florida
Copyright © Karen Fuller 2014
Hardback ISBN: 9781629892320
Print ISBN: 9781629890784
E-Book ISBN: 9781629890791
First Edition World Castle Publishing, LLC, March 28, 2014
http://www.worldcastlepublishing.com

Licensing Notes

Cover: Karen Fuller
Editor: Maxine Bringenberg

CHAPTER ONE

They say things happen for a reason. Amanda Archer had always been a firm believer in that. She never boasted that she knew the whys or hows of it, but what she did know was that her descent into the darkness began two days before she met Marco.

She thought she had it all. She was twenty-five, had a top-paying job that she loved as an advertising executive, and lived in a trendy upscale apartment with a hot boyfriend that her friends just drooled over. Yep, she thought she had it all....

Hearing a soft knock on her office door, Amanda looked up from the computer screen and saw her best friend and coworker, Caroline, shadowing the opening. Caroline wore the black dress pants and white long-sleeved blouse that was the signature uniform trademark of Glasko Advertising Agency, their employer. Amanda paused in the greeting she was about to utter when she noticed the expression on her friend's face. Caroline looked as though she were ready to burst with excitement, with a huge smile splitting her petite face and her lively eyes dancing. Clutched in her trembling fingers was an impressive beige envelope. Her excitement was contagious, and Amanda couldn't help but smile back as she rolled her chair away from her desk. "What's going on?"

Caroline rolled her eyes, bouncing on the balls of her feet. "You'll never guess what I'm holding in my hands, Amanda."

Amanda laughed softly. "No, but you're going to tell me, right?"

Caroline squealed happily, bouncing on her feet again. "We got it, girl!"

Amanda caught her breath, clenching her fists in anticipation. "Please tell me you're talking about the advertising project we've been busting our butts on." Caroline nodded frantically. Throwing her arms wide, Amanda laughed excitedly. "Yes! Thank you, God!"

She sprung out of her chair, and Caroline flung herself into Amanda's arms. "We did it. We did it. We did it!" Caroline squealed again as they jumped up and down in a circle. Letting go, Caroline backed away and spoke. "Charlie and Ray don't know yet."

"Let me guess…we're on our way to rub their noses in it, right?"

"You better believe it!"

"You know they're going to be pissed."

"I'm counting on it."

"Girl, you're so bad."

Caroline nodded as another giggle erupted. "Charlie's an ass, and you know it." Amanda nodded, and Caroline continued. "And Ray…well, Ray…uh…he's just…you know…." Caroline shrugged, scrunching up her face. "Ray."

She dropped her voice an octave. "B-o-r-i-n-g."

Amanda shook her head, snickering at her theatrics. "Caroline. That's not very nice. You know very well that Ray's a nice guy."

Caroline threw her head back, laughing harder. "Yeah, well, he gets a bunch of points taken away for just hanging out with Charlie."

"I heard that!"

Amanda's eyes widened, her gaze darting to the doorway. "Charlie...uh...how long have you been standing there?"

Crossing his arms over his chest, Charlie narrowed his slate-blue eyes to glare at them. Ruggedly handsome with a square jaw and straight nose, he wore his blond hair cropped close at the sides but long on top, falling rakishly across his forehead. He wore a long-sleeved white dress shirt with a black tie and black dress pants. Setting his jaw in irritation, he grumbled, "Long enough."

Caroline giggled again, causing Charlie's glare to intensify, and she rolled her eyes. "Ah, come on, Charlie. It's just a little inner office rivalry. Get over yourself."

He lifted an eyebrow. "How can knocking off points for hanging out with me be 'just a little inner office rivalry'?"

Amanda elbowed Caroline in the ribs and whispered, "He hasn't heard the news yet?"

He glared into Amanda's eyes. "News?"

Caroline shrugged, whispering back, "I told you that they didn't know yet."

Amanda frowned at her and grumbled, "Great." Caroline's smile grew as she shrugged her shoulders again, and this time Amanda rolled her eyes. She turned back to Charlie, pasting on an over-bright smile. "Yes, news, Charlie. You see, Caroline and I were awarded the De Lucia project."

He scowled, throwing out his hands in exasperation. "You've got to be fucking kidding me! What did you two do, fuck Walter?"

Amanda's eyes widened. *He did not just go there.* "Sure, Charlie. We had a real fucking orgy with Walter. It was a blast." When he gave her a satisfied smirk, she rolled her eyes again. "No…Charlie, you know, you're such an ass! Don't be stupid. We didn't sleep with Walter, and I don't kid about work assignments." She gazed past him, searching the hallway, checking to see if anyone had overheard his outburst. "You need to watch your language in the office, Charlie. You know Walter could be around the corner within earshot. Besides, we earned the job fair and square."

Amanda caught Caroline's wince out of the corner of her eye. Charlie honed in on it, narrowing his eyes again, and demanded, "Do you know something we don't know that you're not sharing, Caroline?"

She managed a weak shrug. "Mr. De Lucia insisted on having Amanda on the project. He told Walter that if Amanda wasn't in charge, then Glasko Advertising wouldn't get the contract. Walter readily agreed because, after all, it is a multi-million dollar project."

Amanda's jaw dropped slack at her words.

Charlie sharpened his glare on Amanda. "So, *you* are fucking Mr. De Lucia."

She glared back, setting her jaw. "Charlie, I don't even *know* Mr. De Lucia. I don't even know what he looks like."

She glanced at Caroline, her voice dropping to a whisper. "There's got to be some mistake. He insisted that I head the project?"

Caroline nodded. "He sure did, kiddo. It looks like you're a hot commodity."

Amanda felt a lump grow in her throat; she swallowed hard to get past it. "No pressure there."

Caroline smiled again. "Look at it this way...Mr. De Lucia doesn't seem to think you can do anything wrong." Lifting her hand, she mock punched Amanda on the shoulder. "Milk it for all it's worth, kiddo!" She reached over, looping her arm through Amanda's, and tugged.

Amanda hesitated. "Where are we going?"

She winked playfully. "Did you forget that this project comes with perks? We now have penthouse offices." She tugged again, and this time Amanda followed. "See you later, Charlie."

He shoved his hands into his pockets. "This isn't over."

~*~

Amanda pushed the "P" button in the elevator for the penthouse. It seemed strange to be going to see her new office on the penthouse floor. The only other people who had offices up there were the owners of Glasko Advertising Agency, John and Margo Glasko, and of course, Walter. Now they could add hers and Caroline's names to that exclusive list.

"Amanda, you've got that look."

"Caroline, stop. I don't have any particular kind of look."

"Yeah, you do. You look like you're thinking about walking into Walter's office and refusing the job. I will tell you that you can forget that notion. Mr. De Lucia said there would be no account if you're not on it, so—"

Amanda sighed. "If I want to keep my job, then I'll accept the account."

"You see? I knew that you had the brains to make top executive."

"Yeah, yeah, yeah...."

Once the elevator doors opened, they stepped out into a spacious entrance. A huge mahogany office station was positioned in the center, housing a receptionist exclusive to that floor. Their friend Stacy had landed that cushy job about two years ago.

Stacey's face split into a grin as Caroline and Amanda stepped off the elevator. She placed the phone back on the receiver, motioning them over to her workstation. "Look who decided to join me in the penthouse."

Amanda laughed. "Hi, Stacey. Yeah, it looks like we're all going to be up here together."

"I'm so glad they finally told you two about the job because I've known all week, and I've been about to bust."

Caroline's mouth gaped. "All week?"

"Yep. They've been redecorating and putting lettering on the doors and everything."

Amanda suddenly felt uneasy. "Huh—that's weird. Walter doesn't have his name on his door. Why us?"

Stacey shrugged. "Mr. De Lucia insisted, and what Mr. De Lucia wants, Mr. Lucia...."

"...gets." Stacey nodded as Amanda finished for her.

"Amanda!"

She jumped at Caroline's reprimand. "What...?"

"You're doing it again. Get that 'look' off your face and just accept that good things do happen."

"I'm sorry. I can't help it."

"You *can* help it. Your salary's being doubled. If you can't be happy about anything else, then be happy about that."

Caroline was right. Anybody else would be ecstatic about the promotion. It was just something about the way Amanda got it that put her nerves on edge. She had always worked hard, earning everything that she had achieved. She didn't even know the man that insisted that she head the job. She'd never even seen him. It just felt...*creepy*.

Amanda smiled weakly at Caroline. "I guess you're right."

Caroline huffed, "Girl, you need to see a shrink." Then she smiled. "With that fat new paycheck, you'll now be able to afford one."

"Haha, very funny."

Stacey chimed in. "Amanda, I don't see what your problem is about Mr. Dreamy. He seems like a nice man."

Amanda raised an eyebrow at Stacey. "Mr. Dreamy?"

She wiggled her eyebrows. "You know. Mr. De Lucia—Mr. D-r-e-a-m-y."

Now she had Amanda's attention. "You've seen the elusive Mr. De Lucia?"

Her toothy smile grew. "Yep."

Amanda stared at her. "And?"

"And what?"

Caroline sat on the edge of Stacey's desk, leaning toward her. "Spill, Stacey. You can't drop a huge hint like Mr.

D-r-e-a-m-y and leave it at that."

She nodded. "Sure, I can."

"Stacey!" Caroline snapped, and Stacey jumped. Amanda couldn't help but laugh at the two of them.

"Oh, alright! Geez, can't a girl have a little fun?" She sat back in her chair and gave her friends an exaggerated sigh. "He looks Italian, but I suppose with the last name of De Lucia, he would have to be. It even sounds Italian. You know the type. Dark complexion, ruggedly handsome features, jet black hair. He's tall, about 6'5". The way he fills out that Armani suit...mmm...." She wiggled her eyebrows again. "Hard not to stare at that tight ass as he walks away. He's got the entire package." She leaned forward, putting her elbows on her desk. "Amanda, he makes Jeffrey pale in comparison, and you know that I think your Jeffrey is totally hot."

It was common knowledge that both Stacey and Caroline thought Amanda's boyfriend, Jeffrey, was hot. Sometimes she had the feeling that she'd better not leave them in the room alone with him for too long.

Glancing over at Caroline, Amanda smirked. "I think she's feeding us a line. He's probably short and dumpy."

Stacey sat back in her chair again and splayed her hands. "What, you don't believe me?"

"Let's just say I think you are exaggerating a bit."

"You'll find out soon enough."

"I'm sure we will," Amanda mumbled to herself.

Caroline shook her head at Amanda as she stood back up. "Behave," she whispered in Amanda's direction, then spoke louder for Stacey's benefit. "Stacey, we'll catch you in a few. We're going to check out our new offices."

"Stop nagging," Amanda whispered back.

"You know where I'll be." Stacey gave a secretive smile as she turned back to her computer monitors. "Oh, if someone calls, ring them through or take a message?"

"Ring them through," Amanda said over her shoulder as she headed toward her new office.

~*~

As Amanda entered the newly decorated office and looked around, taking everything in, a small smile formed on her lips. The room was fantastic…everything was shiny and new. The walls were papered in lavish beige linen and lined with magnificent, vibrant oil paintings. A huge desk, deep mahogany, sat in the center of the room. On the surface, dual flat-screen computer monitors were placed in the far corner. The keyboard was hidden on a tray under the edge. Amanda's smile grew as she picked up the nameplate and ran her fingers over the elaborate black and gold lettering that read "Amanda Archer, Account Executive." "This can't be really happening," she said as she put the nameplate down and turned around to gawk at the matching bookshelves lining the far wall. Artwork of various types adorned the shelves. She headed in that direction to admire the pieces. Everything, including the oils on the walls, shared a wolf theme. She ran her fingers gently over a medium-sized statue. "Wolf…hum, I never thought of decorating in this theme."

She turned back toward the desk, noticing another smaller set of shelves behind the desk. A basket wrapped in brightly colored cellophane paper caught her eye. Next to it stood a vase with a dozen red roses. She picked up the card, reading the inscription.

Amanda,
I am looking forward to our time working together. Welcome to your new office. I hope that you like it. It was designed specifically with you in mind. Take the rest of the day off to celebrate. Enjoy the wine; it comes from my private stock. You deserve it.
M. De Lucia

Amanda put the note down and opened the cellophane on the basket. Inside was a bottle of red wine, a cheese ball, crackers, and a beef stick. She hefted the bottle out of the basket; it looked to be ancient, with an old-fashioned cork. Squinting her eyes, she read the faded label and caught her breath. The label had a hand-sketched wolf's head and was handwritten in Italian; she couldn't read a word of it…well, except for the date. The imprinted date was 1812. That bottle of wine was probably valued at a month's salary or more. Placing it carefully back in the basket, she smiled. She knew exactly what she was going to do with it. The note said to take the rest of the day off and celebrate. Well, she'd do just that. She'd take the basket home to share it with Jeffrey and celebrate her promotion with an afternoon in bed with her favorite guy. He happened to have the day off, too, so she figured he'd like to share in her celebration.

CHAPTER TWO

Traffic was awful. Traveling through Chicago's downtown business district in the middle of the day was the one thing that Amanda hated about the area. The drive home normally took about fifteen minutes; today, it was forty-five minutes before Amanda reached her apartment on W. Kinzie St. due to a couple of traffic jams.

Parking her Lexus in its reserved spot in the parking garage, she grabbed the basket and headed for the lobby, where she was greeted by Hank, the doorman, when she stepped off the service elevator. His eyes widened when he saw her. "Good afternoon, Miss Archer."

"Hello, Hank."

"It's nice to see you home *so early* today."

His smile appeared cautious, and she thought that odd. Hank was usually a very friendly doorman. He was friends with her boyfriend, Jeffrey, and was usually friendlier to her for just that reason. Something was either weighing on his mind or bothering him. She tried looking into his eyes, and he looked away. *He is definitely avoiding me*, she thought. "Are you okay, Hank?"

He cleared his throat behind a balled fist. "Never better. Can I get the elevator for you?"

"Sure."

He punched the button, and the doors opened. "Have a good afternoon, Miss Archer."

"You too, Hank."

The plush elevator took her up to the apartment on the penthouse floor. As she unlocked the door and stepped inside, she set the basket on the floor just inside the doorway. She placed her purse and keys on the nearby table, then entered the living room. "Jeffrey, I'm home…oh, my God!"

She had decided to surprise Jeffrey by coming home early with the news. Unfortunately, Jeffrey wasn't the only one surprised. Amanda couldn't believe her eyes. She had just caught Jeffrey and the building's slut, Clair, carrying on like a couple of bunnies on the floor in front of the blazing fireplace.

"Amanda! What are you…? You're not supposed to be here!"

"Obviously."

"Amanda, I can expl—"

She held up her hand to stop his speech and rounded on the blonde bimbo on the floor. "Clair, get your scrawny ass up and get out of my apartment!"

"Don't get your panties in a wad. I'm going."

Clair was getting up, but she wasn't moving fast enough to suit Amanda. Amanda bent down, scooped up Clair's clothes, and took a fist full of her bleach-blonde hair, dragging her to the door as Clair screeched in rage. But Clair wasn't half as angry as Amanda was; she shoved Clair's naked butt out the door, throwing her clothes after her.

She slammed the door and turned on Jeffrey. He had managed to slip into a pair of jeans while she was dealing with "the trash." She placed her hands on her hips. "You know, I really thought we had something special, but obviously, I was mistaken."

"Amanda, baby, it wasn't what it looked like."

She couldn't believe her ears. If it hadn't been so pathetic, she would have laughed. "It wasn't what it looked like," she repeated. "*Right*. Oh, and don't call me baby."

"You're upset."

Her mouth gaped. "You think?"

"Yes. If you step back and look at the bigger picture, you will see that she didn't mean anything to me. I love *you*, baby."

She nodded in disbelief. "You want me to look at the bigger picture?"

"Y-e-s!"

"Well, Jeffrey, let me tell *you* something." She jabbed her index finger at his chest. "I did just '*see*' the bigger picture. With my own eyes, I might add. What I saw was you fucking the building's number-one slut. I caught you red-handed with your dick where it ain't supposed to be. And let me tell you right now that I don't want it anywhere near me again. Pack your shit and GET OUT!"

"You can't kick me out!"

"I just did!"

"But—"

"Read my lips, Jeffrey. Get out. I don't *need* you. I *don't want* you anymore."

"Where am I supposed to go?"

"You need somewhere to stay?" He looked away from her and nodded. "Why don't you go ask that bleach-blonde bimbo for a place to stay?"

He shook his head. "I don't want Clair. I want you."

"You should have thought about that before you fucked Clair; now it's too late." She bent down and picked his shirt up off the floor, then threw it at him. "You have thirty minutes before I call security to have you forcibly removed."

Jeffrey didn't own much, mainly his clothes, all of which fit into two large suitcases. Everything else belonged to Amanda: the apartment, the furniture, the checking account, the six-figure income…everything. In that moment, it dawned on her that the only things Jeffrey had going for him were a gorgeous face and a tight body. He was a waiter, and his income barely supported his expensive clothes and jewelry habits. The realization that she might have just been a free meal ticket did nothing but piss her off further.

~*~

She stood on the balcony staring at the water when she heard the front door slam behind her. It was strange. She had really thought she was in love with Jeffrey. They had been together for six months. When she heard that door slam, she should have felt pain and betrayal, but all she felt was relief that he was finally gone. She wasn't happy by any means and was still pretty pissed off, but strangely she didn't shed the first tear over Jeffrey.

With his departure, she entered the apartment again. That's when she remembered the basket by the front door.

Positioning the basket on the kitchen island, she

proceeded to unload it. The cheese ball and the beef stick were put in the refrigerator because her encounter with Jeffrey didn't leave her with much of an appetite. Taking the bottle of wine out of the basket, she cradled it in her hands and stared at it glumly. "This was supposed to be a celebration." The rich, blood-red liquid coating the inside of the bottle beckoned her with the promise of its sweet taste and oblivion. She made a decision that she would still celebrate, albeit by herself. She would celebrate the new job and Jeffrey's departure from her life by tying on a good one.

Amanda broke the seal and poured herself a tall glass of the wine. She took it with her into the living room, stopping briefly to turn on the stereo and pluck a romance novel off the bookshelf. A good book would take her mind off that cheating bastard. Settling on the couch, she tucked her feet beneath her and opened the book.

Absently, she brought the glass to her lips but stopped before she took a sip. The first thing that caught her attention was the odd aroma of the wine. She closed the book and placed it on the coffee table, then sniffed at the wine again. Furrowing her brow, she stared hard at the red liquid, then took a small taste. The flavor was sweet and sumptuous as it rolled over her tongue, but it had a slight metallic taste as well that she couldn't identify. Having never tasted a wine that was two hundred years old, she attributed the oddities to the advanced age, then took a deep swallow. Instantly warmth permeated her body, causing her to smile. *This is just what the good doctor ordered*, she thought, then tipped the glass and drained it.

The second glass went down almost as quickly as the

first. She set the glass on the table and leaned back into the couch's cushions. A feeling of fire coursed through her body, lapping at her skin. Every nerve ending was hypersensitive, and she was shocked to find that she was sexually aroused. Running her fingers lightly between her legs, she nearly cried out at the throbbing and heightened sensations the light touch caused.

Fear engulfed her as she was suddenly under the very real impression that the bottle of wine was laced with something. Her heartbeat picked up to a maddening pace as her skin grew hotter with each passing second, and the ache between her legs became nearly unbearable. She was now trembling with a need so great she was nearly mindless.

"Whoa, this is fucked up." Her tongue felt thick, and her words sounded slurred to her own ears. "Think…think. You're not drunk. You've never been drunk on two glasses of wine before. Someone must have put something in the wine…but they couldn't have. You broke the seal. The bottle hadn't been tampered with…unless…." Swallowing hard, she tried to focus as the room swam in her vision. "Unless it was done two hundred years ago. This'll pass. It's gotta pass, girl. Just remain calm. The man wouldn't poison you…at least not on purpose. You're his star player, right?" Confused and frightened, she decided to lie down on the couch until it passed. She was dizzy and trembling so badly she was afraid to try to walk across the room to get to the phone to call for help.

As she settled on the plush cushions, she felt the heat surging through her body, becoming almost unbearable. Absently she unbuttoned her shirt and closed her eyes, and things grew a little fuzzy.

The room spun as flashes of light danced behind her eyelids. Visions of hypnotic golden eyes glowed intently, seeming to devour her, and then were gone. Then the visions turned to unknown couples engaged in an orgy of frenzied sex. Fascinated, her mind's eye couldn't look away. Watching the writhing bodies, each pleasuring the other, was the most erotic thing she'd ever witnessed, causing the ache between her own legs to grow. She had never had these types of fantasies before and felt the fluid gush from her core. To her surprise and horror, as each of the rutting couples yelled out in climax, they transformed into mating wolves.

Feeling a presence in the room, Amanda tried to open her eyes from her vivid dream, but they wouldn't obey her mental command. In fact, she couldn't move a muscle on her own without great effort. Her arms and legs felt like leaded weights, and the effort to move was just too much. Her heart raced, and the now constant burning between her legs throbbed with renewed force.

Unexpectedly she felt the velvet touch of fevered hands as they traveled across her body, touching her everywhere, leaving a scorching path and a deeper yearning in their wake. She felt the tugging of fabric and the cooler air as each item of her clothing seemed to vanish. With her now naked and exposed, the hands resumed the exploration of her body as if they worshiped her, stroking and kneading as they went. She felt the caresses stop at her thighs, then gently force them apart. Her muddled mind had no will to fight or even want them to stop. The only sound she emitted was a moan of need as she felt the fingers between her legs, opening her folds to easily slip inside.

Her restless mind warred between reality and dream. She certainly felt that she had to be dreaming because she was in her apartment, alone, with the front door bolted. Surely this had to be a dream, so she let go and allowed her body to respond and just feel. The fingers skillfully moved in and out in rhythm as her body wreathed and bucked for more, bringing her higher with each tender stroke, her body responding to *his* commands, not her own. She thought she heard a soft chuckle, but her mind attributed it to the erotic dream.

She felt soft lips circle one of her nipples, eagerly sucking, with a hot tongue laving and kneading the marbled peak. Instinctively arching her back, she tried to get closer to the source. Her passions were nearly cresting when she heard a soft, masculine, heavily accented voice…. "Not yet."

She felt the fingers withdraw and wanted to yell, "No, not yet," but the only noise she made was a soft whimper. She felt a mouth cover hers in a soft yet demanding kiss. His tongue slipped between her eager lips to explore and drive her further mad with want. She lifted her leaded arms, drawing him closer, running her fingers through his silken locks. His sweet, spicy scent added to the maddening illusion.

Then, Amanda felt hot bare skin touch hers as his body eased over her and between her legs. The intoxicating kiss continued as she felt the firm, soft head of his cock at her tender folds. Instinctively, she spread her legs wider. His lips withdrew from hers, and she heard a soft, "Yes, Amanda, open to me." She briefly wondered how her dream lover knew her name, and then he gripped her hips with his hands and fully impaled her with one firm thrust of his engorged staff, filling and stretching her. He ground his hips to hers, giving a triumphant roar, then said, "You are mine."

Her mind succumbed to sensation, her body took over, and her voice spoke of its own accord, "Yes." Amanda's fevered body wanted him to move. Her hips bucked at his, but his firm grip held her still.

"Say it. Say the words to me. Pledge yourself to me."

His heavily accented words confused her. Amanda only wanted him to move to ease her aching loins.

"Say it!"

"I—I am yours."

"Yes. Now the prophecy will be fulfilled."

Her numb mind raced. *Prophecy? What prophecy?* And then he rocked his hips, and her mind was lost once again in pure sensation.

He withdrew only to thrust again, over and over, taking her higher, burying his cock to the hilt with each plunge. Her body greedily accepted his as she wrapped her legs around his hips, their bodies thrashing as one. His teeth nipped at her budded nipples as she writhed beneath him in mindless passion. With one strong final thrust and a slight sting in her left shoulder, she lost herself as millions of lights exploded behind her eyelids, and her body shuddered violently, pulsating around him, milking him in a powerful release as they came together. The last thing she remembered was his roar of triumph when everything went black.

CHAPTER THREE

The shrill ring of Amanda's cell phone woke her. She sat up on the couch, grabbing her head between the palms of her hands as a new wave of dizziness engulfed her. The high-pitched ring bounced off her eardrums, and she struggled to cover her ears with the palms of her hands to block the sound. It rang once more, then stopped. Cautiously lowering her hands, she righted herself on the couch. Memories of the night before flooded back to her as she peeled an eye open, warily looking down at herself, and was relieved to find herself fully dressed. *It was just a dream*, she thought. Looking around the room, she didn't notice anything out of place. A quick glance at the door confirmed that it was indeed bolted and chained. A peek at the terrace confirmed that the door was closed. The sky was black behind the curtains, so she assumed it was night.

For the first time since she opened the bottle of wine, she breathed a sigh of relief, smiling to herself. *That was some erotic dream you had*, she thought as her body warmed to the memory. Her mind was clearing quickly, and she realized that it had to be a dream. She had never had sex that incredible in her life, and she could only dream up something that bizarre and erotic.

The cell phone rang again, and she winced as the sound pierced her skull. "Ah, stop ringing. You're killing me," she cried out as she stumbled to her feet. "Where are you?" She had left it on the island in the kitchen. She reached it by the third ring. "Hello?"

"Amanda—thank God. Where have you been?"

"Caroline, what do you mean? Where have I been? I've been home. Where do you think?"

"Well, I thought that you must be on your deathbed. You didn't show up for work. I called Jeffrey, and he said you kicked him out. I banged on your door at lunch and must have called you at least a million times."

Her mouth gaped in disbelief. "I only took a nap. I haven't missed work."

"Think again, kiddo. You left early yesterday, and no one has seen you since."

Amanda laughed. "Did Jeffrey put you up to this to get back at me?"

"This is no joke. You scared me to death, Amanda. Especially when Jeffrey said you kicked him out. I thought you might have done something drastic—why did you kick him out?"

Amanda scoffed. "He didn't tell you?"

"Uh—no, why?"

"Caroline, your voice sounds funny." She looked at the phone, frowning. "You didn't let Jeffrey stay with you, did you?"

"Well—I didn't figure you'd care if you kicked him out."

Amanda rolled her eyes. "You know what? You can have him."

"You mean it?"

"Absolutely. I don't want that dick back."

"Hey, that's not being very nice."

"He's there with you now, isn't he?"

"Uh, yeah...."

"Ask him why I kicked him out. Let's see if he'll tell you the truth."

"Okay, hang on." Amanda heard a muffled conversation. "He got pissed and stormed out of the room."

"He didn't tell you?"

"Nope."

"It figures, the little prick. I came home early yesterday and caught him red-handed fucking Clair in front of the fireplace. In my own living room. He's a freeloading, cheating bastard. If you want to take him in, then do it with your eyes open. I'm through with him."

"That must have been awful."

"It was, but you know, it was kind of a relief too. It was like a weight lifted from my shoulders when he left."

"If that was the case, then why didn't you come to work today or answer the phone?"

"I can't explain it. I only had a couple of glasses of wine. I got dizzy and either fell asleep or passed out. I had an erotic dream, then the phone woke me up when you called."

"Erotic dream...what did the hunk look like?"

Amanda laughed. "I haven't a clue. The dream was very weird. It almost felt like it was real. I couldn't open my eyes and see him, but that somehow added to the excitement.

I don't know. Anyway, I think it must have had some spin-off of what Stacy said earlier today — er, yesterday, or whatever when she teased us about Mr. De Lucia because the guy in my dream had a thick Italian accent."

Caroline laughed with her. "Here you are at work worrying about Mr. De Lucia insisting you have the job, and you're having sexual dreams about the man, for Christ's sake."

"So, sue me."

"Nah — it will be more fun to tease you when you actually do see him."

"What do you mean?"

"What I mean is Stacey was understating the man. I had to pick my jaw up off the floor and wipe the drool off my chin. I kid you not. I don't know how I'm going to get any work done if he's in the room, or even on the same floor for that matter."

"I'm sorry I missed it."

"You should be. He didn't look too happy that you weren't at work."

Amanda winced. "It's his fault. He's the one that gave me the bottle of wine with a personal note to enjoy it. I was just following his instructions. I didn't have any intention of passing out on the couch." She picked up the bottle and looked at it. "That's strange. Looking at the level mark on the bottle, it doesn't even look like I've had a full glass, much less two glasses. Huh…I'm not usually such a lightweight."

"That is strange. You can usually hold your own when we party."

"Maybe the bottle of wine being two hundred years

old has something to do with it."

"He gave you a two-hundred-year-old bottle of wine?"

"Yeah, that's what the label says anyway."

"Wow…but that's not the point. I don't think the age has anything to do with potency. Did you uh…take anything recreational with it?"

Amanda scowled at the phone. "You know very well that I don't do drugs."

"Sorry, just checking. You don't normally sleep through twenty-four hours, either. I'm just worried about you, that's all."

"I know. I'm sorry if I snapped at you. Anyway, let me go. Now that I'm up, I'm about to starve, and I'm going to fix myself something to eat."

"Do you mind if I come over and see with my own eyes that you're okay?"

"Suit yourself."

"Good. I'll see you in a bit."

"Alright. Have you eaten? If not, I can fix you something too."

"Yeah—Jeffrey and I ate about an hour ago. I'll see you in a few minutes."

"Caroline, be sure you come alone. I don't want to see Jeffrey for a good long while, if ever."

"Okay…I'll come alone, but you're going to have to see him sometime."

Amanda rolled her eyes at the phone. "Goodbye, Caroline."

~*~

Amanda sat down to eat a steak and baked potato. She

was nearly half finished eating when there was a knock at the door.

Amanda opened the door, and there stood Caroline, biting her lip, with worry creasing her brow. Amanda smiled at her friend, then motioned her to follow. "Hey girl, I'm at the table in the kitchen eating. Do you want something to drink?"

Caroline followed Amanda back to the kitchen. "I'll get it myself. You eat."

Caroline grabbed a Diet Coke from the refrigerator while Amanda sat back down to resume eating. Amanda had the next bite nearly to her mouth when Caroline grabbed her hand and yelled, "What the hell do you think you're eating?"

"Steak, what does it look like?" Amanda said sarcastically.

Caroline winced. "Since when do you eat raw meat?"

Amanda rolled her eyes. "It's not raw. It's just...." She looked at her fork, and her eyes widened. She then looked down at her plate. "...raw." The other half of the steak remained on the plate in a puddle of blood. She let the fork drop to the plate with the uneaten meat still attached. "I think I'm going to be sick."

Caroline placed her hand on Amanda's forehead. "Maybe you *are* sick and just don't know it. Maybe I should take you to the E.R. Your head feels hot."

Amanda jerked away from her hand, clearly irritated. "I'm fine." She took out a pan and dumped the remainder of the steak from the plate into it.

"Boy, you sure are grouchy today."

"You would be too."

"Okay, okay. I get your point." Caroline leaned her hip

against the counter as she watched Amanda cook the steak. "You're still going to eat that?"

"Yeah, I'm still about to starve. Why not?"

She pointed to the steak in the pan. "I would have figured that would have upset your stomach."

"I would have thought so, too, but it didn't. So I intend to eat the rest of it. It's not like it was spoiled or anything. Just a little undercooked."

"Undercooked? That thing was raw."

Amanda poked the sizzling meat with a fork. "Just a technicality."

"What do you mean 'just a technicality'? That thing was raw."

Amanda jabbed the fork into the undercooked steak, putting it back on the plate.

Caroline made a face. "It's still raw."

Amanda shrugged. "That's as done as it's going to get. The smell of it cooking is turning my stomach a little. It smelled better the other way."

Caroline's mouth gaped as she watched Amanda sit back down at the table and continue to eat. "That is totally disgusting."

Amanda put her fork down and glared at her friend. "If you don't like to watch me eat, then don't watch! Geez! I'm craving this for some reason."

"Amanda — you're not...."

"Not what?" Amanda popped another bite of steak in her mouth and chewed warily as she watched Caroline carefully.

Caroline pulled out a chair and sat down, placing her

elbows on the table. "You know…pregnant?"

Amanda stopped mid-chew, raising both eyebrows in disbelief. Caroline nodded, then Amanda swallowed the meat. "Excuse me?"

Caroline sat back in her seat. "Well, you've got to admit that is one hell of a craving you've got there."

Amanda scoffed. "I will admit that even I think this craving is strange, but I'm pretty sure I'm not pregnant."

Caroline cocked her head to the side. "Oh? You and Jeffrey lived together for six months."

Amanda scowled. "Don't remind me. No, I'm still pretty sure that I'm not pregnant. I better not be. Jeffrey will be so unhappy if I am." Caroline shrugged at that remark, and Amanda continued, "Maybe I'm just anemic or something."

Caroline smiled wickedly. "Maybe you're turning into a vampire."

Amanda thought back to her weird dream, and her heart dropped. Then she really thought about it and dismissed it totally because, after all, it was only a dream. "That's cute, Caroline. I like that. What do you do for an encore?"

Caroline giggled. "Chill-lax, girl. I'm just messing with you." She pointed to the plate. "I don't know what the craving for that is…." She shivered in revulsion, then continued. "But that's you. It's not me. If you want to eat your food that way… go for it." She smiled teasingly. "We're still friends, even if you have turned into a vampire."

Amanda grinned, then swatted at her arm. "Shut up!"

"I'm just saying…."

"Stop messing with me and answer your phone."

"My phone's not ringing."

Amanda distinctly heard a phone ringing. "This is the sixth ring. Just answer the damn thing."

Caroline reached inside her purse, retrieving her phone and held it out. "See, it's not me."

Amanda cocked her head to the side and listened. She heard someone answer the phone, then caught a startled breath when she realized who it was. The voice was Clair's... but that was impossible. Clair lived six floors down.

"Amanda, what's wrong?"

Amanda held up her hand to stop Caroline's questions and listened harder. *"Hi, Jeffrey…. Yeah, I'm sorry too. I hate she caught us like that. Bummer…. No, no, I'm not busy…. Come on over. I'll put on something sexy and wait on you…. Great, I'll see you in about twenty minutes. Bye."* Amanda heard the audible click of the phone disconnecting.

Amanda closed her eyes, mumbling under her breath, "That no-good cheating bastard."

Caroline placed her hand over Amanda's and squeezed to get her attention back. "Who's a cheating bastard?"

Amanda's eyes locked with Caroline's. "Jeffrey."

Caroline sighed heavily. "I know he hurt you. You said earlier that it was a relief that he's gone. I don't know why you're dwelling on it so much if he didn't mean that much to you."

"Caroline, this time, I didn't call him a cheating bastard on my behalf. He's at it again."

Caroline's mouth gaped. "What?"

Amanda nodded. "He's at it again."

"I don't understand. How would you know?"

Amanda rose from the table, heading for the front

door. She opened it, sticking her head out in the hallway, looking both ways. Empty. She closed the door, turning back to Caroline.

"I can't really explain it, but I just heard Clair on the phone, and she spoke to him by name. He's on his way over to her apartment now, and I distinctly heard her say that she was going to put on something sexy for him."

"That no-good cheating bastard." Caroline paused, then shook her head. "Wait a minute. Clair doesn't live on this floor. Was she out in the hallway or something?"

Amanda shrugged. "I looked, but I didn't see her. I don't know, but I distinctly heard her talking on the phone."

Caroline narrowed her eyes. "Raw meat, a whacked-up sense of smell, and now keen hearing. Hmmm…I'm still leaning toward the vampire theory."

"Would you stop?"

Caroline shrugged. "What? You've got to admit, girlfriend, none of this is normal."

"Give me a break. I just have a hangover or something."

"Or something…."

"Caroline."

"I'm just saying…."

"Fine, I'll prove to you that I'm not making any of this up."

Caroline crossed her arms over her chest. "How?"

Amanda gestured to the drawn curtains. "My balcony overlooks the road coming from your house."

"So?"

"We'll stand on the balcony and watch for Jeffrey to drive up. You only live ten minutes from here. If my theory is correct, Jeffrey will drive up within the next ten minutes to take Clair up on her offer."

"I hope you're wrong."

Amanda crossed her arms over her chest, leaning against the counter. "I'm not."

Caroline huffed, then marched over to the drawn curtains, threw them back, and slid open the glass door. The cool night air rushed in, sending the curtains billowing into the room. She took a deep breath, then stepped out onto the balcony. Amanda crossed the threshold behind her. Without looking back, Caroline said, "For Jeffrey's sake, you had better be wrong."

"What if I'm not?"

"If you're not, then I'm kicking him out too."

Amanda smiled. "Good girl."

CHAPTER FOUR

As soon as Amanda arrived at the office building, she headed for the break room and poured herself a cup of coffee. The steaming cup was halfway to her lips when she heard steady, purposeful hand clapping.

She turned and saw Charlie behind her with a shit-eating grin, clapping his hands together.

"What?"

"Way to go, Amanda. You fucked up royally. It was your first day too." He clapped louder. "Bravo."

"Shut up, Charlie. It wasn't my fault."

"Tell that to your new boss." He splayed his hands. "I can see it now…my new office in the penthouse when you get busted down. Thank you for screwing up and giving me this wonderful opportunity."

"I wouldn't be moving my things upstairs yet, dickhead."

He wagged his finger at her. "You're the one who better not be getting too comfortable. Try not to cry too hard. It's not very becoming in an office."

Amanda tilted her head forward, narrowed her eyes,

and growled.

Charlie took a step back in surprise. "Did you just growl at me?"

She looked away and saw Caroline standing in the doorway, shaking her head, indicating not to say anything more to Charlie. She shrugged at Caroline and then looked back at Charlie. "I, uh, don't know what came over me."

"That's okay, Amanda. We both know that your growl is worse than your bite."

She raised her brow, and her upper lip curled back in a snarl.

"Whoa, are you wearing some fancy contacts or something? There is something seriously wrong with your eyes."

Caroline barged into the break room, taking Amanda by the shoulders and shaking her a bit. "Amanda," she whispered harshly, drawing Amanda's glare away from Charlie. "Don't. This asshole's not worth getting fired over. Let's go. Stacey will have coffee ready upstairs."

Amanda nodded, grabbing her purse from the counter, leaving her untouched coffee behind.

Caroline gave Charlie a little shove out of the way. "Leave her alone, Charlie. Mr. De Lucia won't like it, and then *you* will be looking for another job, not Amanda. Go back to the hole you just slithered from."

"This isn't over."

~*~

As soon as the elevator doors closed, Caroline rounded on Amanda. "What the fuck was that all about?"

Amanda glared at her friend. "Don't take your

aggravation at Jeffrey out on me. I warned you that he was a cheating bastard."

Caroline sighed. "This has nothing to do with Jeffrey. I'm worried about *you*. What happened back there?"

Amanda looked down at the floor. "I—I don't know."

"What do you mean you don't know?"

Amanda shrugged helplessly. "Something just came over me when Charlie pissed me off." She shook her head. "I can't explain it. I suddenly saw red, and the next thing I knew, I was growling and then snarling at Charlie."

"I don't know what to think of your strange behavior, girlfriend. I *know* you're not a vampire because you walked out into the sunshine, and you're still here and not a crispy critter." Amanda gave her a small smile. "Don't laugh, Amanda, I was kidding about the vampire thing, but I still think something is seriously wrong with you."

"Me too. My senses are in overdrive. I think Charlie pissed on himself when I snarled at him."

Caroline giggled. "Seriously?"

Amanda nodded. "Yes, I could smell it."

"Yuck, too much information."

"You're telling me. It'll take me a week to get that stench out of my nose."

"Maybe you should just call in sick and try again tomorrow."

Amanda shook her head as the elevator doors opened on the penthouse floor. "No, it's now or never. Whatever has come over me, I'll just have to learn to live with. In the meantime, just please don't let me do anything stupid."

"I'll try, but you really are acting weird. I hope Mr. De

Lucia doesn't notice."

Stacey smiled as they approached her workstation. "Amanda…it's good to see you today. I was worried abo—"

"Coffee, two sugars, one cream."

The smile dropped from Stacey's face as she looked to Caroline for confirmation.

"Did I stutter?" Amanda growled.

"No—I—right away, Miss Archer."

Caroline took Amanda by the shoulders and rushed her into Amanda's office, closing the door behind them. "You did it again. Stop it before you get us both fired."

Amanda plopped down in her chair, splaying her hands. "What? What did I say? I only asked for a cup of coffee."

"Seriously?" Amanda nodded as Caroline plopped down in a chair on the other side of the desk. "Think again, girl. You didn't ask for a cup of coffee. You demanded it, and not very nicely either. I bet poor Stacey's in tears about now."

"No, Stacey's my friend. She knows me better than that."

"You think so?"

"Yes."

"Okay," Caroline said as she leaned forward in her chair to make her point. "Then tell me this. When have you ever known Stacey to call you Miss Archer?"

Amanda tilted her head, giving the question some thought. "Never."

Caroline smirked as she sat back in her chair. "Well, she just did."

"I should apologize."

"Yes, you should."

Amanda grabbed her purse. "Maybe this wasn't such a good idea after all. Maybe I *should* call in sick and go back home."

The intercom buzzed as Caroline opened her mouth to reply. "Miss Archer?"

"Yes, Stacey…uh, I'm sorry."

Stacey sniffed. "Miss Archer, Mr. De Lucia wants to see you in his office…now."

"Uh, oh. Too late now," Caroline said under her breath. "Just don't be rude to Mr. De Lucia, and it'll be fine."

"Thank you, Stacey. Tell him that I'll be right there."

"Yes, Miss Archer, right away."

~*~

Amanda stood outside Mr. De Lucia's closed door, trying to put her thoughts together.

"*Entri Benvenuto, Amanda, si prega di avere un posto a sedere.*"

Amanda felt a moment of panic. "Huh?" she managed to squeak. "Uh, I mean, pardon me?"

She heard him chuckle softly through the closed door, and the sound reminded her of the man in her dream. The memory sent goosebumps up her arm.

"I said, 'Come in. Welcome, Amanda, please have a seat.'"

Maybe it wasn't a dream, she thought. *That voice* is *the same. But that's impossible…or is it? What do I do now?*

"What do you do? You *do* as you're instructed, *tesoro*. *Entri* now, *per favore*…please."

Did he just hear my thoughts?

"I am not accustomed to repeating myself, *tesoro*."

"Yes, sir," she said as she twisted the knob and pushed the door open. "I'm sorry. I haven't been myself today. It's been a weird two days, actually. I—" Her train of thought fled as her gaze now rested on the elusive Mr. De Lucia.

The eyes, they are the same eyes in my dream, but how? Forget the eyes, and don't be stupid, Amanda. You need to look at the total picture. Stacey wasn't exaggerating, she thought. *The man's gorgeous.* He smiled as if he heard her thoughts, flashing perfectly straight white teeth, and she felt her heart flutter. His features were classic Italian…firm jaw, straight nose, well defined lips, black wavy hair framed his face, and he sported a slight five o'clock shadow. As he stood, he held out his hand to her. The man was tall, well over six feet, as Stacey had said. The dark grey Armani suit fit well and accentuated his muscles. Her gaze caught a glint of gold from his left hand pinkie finger. The ring was a snarling wolf with rubies for eyes.

"Do I measure up?"

Startled, she only half heard what he said. "I'm sorry, what?" Her gaze met his.

"You are staring. Do I measure up, *tesoro*?"

She felt the heat rise to her cheeks. "I'm sorry, that was rude of me," she said as she reached for his outstretched hand. "I'm not normally this flustered…it's a pleasure to finally meet you, Mr. De Lucia."

"Marco," he said as his hand enveloped her smaller one. His touch sent sensations up her arm, causing her eyes to widen. "Think nothing of it. It is nice to be regarded so well by a *bella donna*. Please, be seated." He let go of her hand

and leaned on the edge of his desk while she sat in the chair. He crossed his arms over his chest and regarded her. "I trust you're feeling better?"

"Feeling better?"

"You missed work yesterday."

"Oh, that." She looked away. "I wasn't sick...I can't really explain it."

"Do you make a habit of missing work?"

She looked back at him sharply, emitting a low growl. "Certainly not!"

He laughed softly. "Good, good!" he said as he clapped his hands together once. "You *do* have some spirit, after all. You're not the timid mouse you just portrayed yourself to be."

Amanda blinked in shock. "But...but I just growled at you. I'm sorry, I...I don't know what came over me."

Marco pushed away from the desk, then took her hands in his. "Do not apologize for being yourself *il mio amore*. You hide your passion deep within yourself, but I can see it there, the *alfa lupo*, begging to surface. I can sense her calling to mine. Do not be afraid to be yourself around me. *Eravamo fatti per stare insieme, il mio amore.*"

"I don't speak Italian, Marco, so I don't understand. What is an *alfa lu* — ?"

He squeezed her hands, then let go and leaned back against the desk. "*Alfa lupo* is alpha wolf."

Alpha wolf, what in the hell is that supposed to mean? And what does he mean, mine calls to his? He smiled again as if he heard her thoughts. *Did he just read my thoughts?* The smile broadened. She narrowed her eyes and slammed her hand down on the arm of the chair. "Tell me what that last sentence you just said means."

"*Eravamo fatti per stare insieme, il mio amore?*" She nodded. "It translates to 'we were meant to be together, my love.'"

She stood, then started backing toward the door. "And *tesoro?*"

"Sweetheart."

Amanda's back slammed against the door as her fingers fumbled for the doorknob. "This, this is sexual harassment. There are laws against this kind of behavior in the workplace."

"Human laws do not concern me, *tesoro.*" He took a step toward her, and she plastered herself further against the door. "And they shouldn't concern you either, *il mio amore.*"

"You talk like you're not human." When he nodded, her eyes bugged. "You're implying that you're *not* human?"

"No, *we* are not."

"*We?*" She swallowed hard.

"You and I...." She shook her head frantically. "I am not a human." He reached up and ran his knuckles gently across her cheek. "Neither are you, *il mio amore.*"

"If you're not human, then what are you?" Her voice was barely a whisper.

"*We* are *lupo*, wolf."

Amanda felt light-headed and swayed on her feet. Marco pulled her into his arms and rubbed his cheek against hers. "*Tu sei la mia anima gemella, Amanda. Ho aspettato 300 anni per la vostra nascita.*" He sighed. "*Scusi.* In English. You are my soul mate, and I have waited three hundred years for your birth."

Amanda pushed away, then sat back down hard in the

chair. "*You* are crazy. *I* am *not* a wolf, and neither are you. Werewolves are myths, stories told to frighten children and the weak-minded."

Marco flashed her another smile. "Stories like this?" His soft brown eyes changed shape, turning golden and emanating a soft glow.

Her own eyes saucered as she cringed in the chair. "This isn't possible."

The smile left his face as he leaned forward and gripped her shoulders, his eyes now normal. "*Never* cower away from me." His tone was forceful and commanding, then softened. "I will not hurt you, and I never meant to frighten you. You just needed a little convincing. Most all myths are based on truths, and this one is very true. We are *lupo, il mio amore.*"

She took a quivering breath. "I am *not* a wolf, and you...I don't know what you —"

"Liar!" he yelled as his grip tightened on her shoulders.

She grit her teeth, emitting a low growl. "I. Do. Not. Lie!"

Marco yanked her out of the chair, then turned her to face the mirror, forcing her to look at herself. "Look at your reflection, Amanda. *See* what I *see* when you are angry." Amanda's mouth dropped open as she gazed at her reflection. "You see, *il mio amore*? Look at your eyes." She reached up and touched her face and then the mirror, her anger turning to disbelief as tears pooled on her bottom lashes. Her eyes glowed like his. "In the beginning, anger will be your trigger for the change. Your hormones will be raging, and you will anger very easily. This will pass, and you *will* learn to control it."

"I…I don't understand what's happening to me." Her voice broke. "This…this is *not* normal." Her gaze met his in the reflection. "Last night, I was eating raw meat and hearing things I couldn't possibly be hearing. This morning I nearly attacked a co-worker over something stupid, and now *this*." The tears spilled from her lashes to course down her face, then her bottom lip quivered. "You're obviously behind all this. What have you done to me? I'm a freak."

Marco gently turned her to face him, cupping her face in the palms of his hands, gazing intently into her eyes. "What have I done to you?" She swallowed hard, then nodded. "I have done nothing but awaken your inner wolf. She has always been there just below the surface…impatiently waiting."

"*She*?" He nodded. "What is '*she*' waiting for?"

The corners of his mouth turned up in a slight smile as he answered. "She *was* waiting to be claimed by me."

Amanda caught her breath. "*Was*?"

"We are a proud and superior race, Amanda." His thumb slid across her cheek, brushing away a tear. "Be proud of who you are. You are not a freak. You are *my* miracle, *il mio compagno*."

"You didn't answer my question."

"You are *mine*, Amanda. You bear my mark." He moved her open collar aside and brushed the marks on her shoulder with his fingertips. Her brow furrowed as she strained to see. She pushed away from him and turned to the mirror, baring her shoulder fully, and glared at the marks in the mirror. "No other would dare touch you."

Amanda lifted her hands and wiped the remaining tears from her cheeks. Her eyes narrowed as she scowled at him in the mirror's reflection, her jaw set, her upper lip curled back in a snarl.

He threw his head back and laughed. "*Tu sei magnifico, il mio amore. Tale fuoco e bellezza.*" (You are magnificent, my love. Such fire and beauty.)

She balled her fists and whirled around to face him. "I'll show you a firey beauty!"

He stopped laughing and regarded her statement, a slight smirk still remaining. "So, you understood what I said?"

"*Sì*," she seethed as she reared back her fist and punched him in the nose.

Marco's eyes widened in surprise as he brought his hand up to cover his nose.

"*Arrogante bastardo!*" she spat as she brought her fist up again to strike. His open palm caught her fist, and he wrenched her hand behind her back, bringing her chest up to his. Her chest heaved against his body as she struggled to free herself. "Let me go, Marco, or I swear to God I *will* hurt you. I can see for myself that you *bleed* like any other man." Even as she spoke the words, the blood faded.

He brought his other hand up and brushed the hair from her eyes. "You cannot hurt me, my little *alfa lupo*. We are mates. It is in our genes that a mate cannot hurt the other." Her mouth dropped open. He smiled. "You see, between mates, the sex can get a little...rough." He shrugged. "Our genetics protect us from unintentional harm from the other."

"How about intentional harm?" she growled as her knee connected with his groin.

He let go of her hand but didn't double over as she had expected. Instead, he wrapped his arms around her and drew her body fully to his. She brought her hands up to push against his chest. "That hurt," he said, his lips a hair's-breadth from hers.

She grinned. "Good. I meant for it to hurt. Now let me go."

Marco quirked an eyebrow, then brought a hand down to cup her ass and brought her hips firmly against his erection. "No."

The smile dropped from Amanda's face as her brow furrowed in disbelief. "That's impossible. I just kneed you there. There is no way —"

His lips covered hers, taking her by surprise and halting her protest in mid-sentence. Amanda's body betrayed her turbulent thoughts by clutching him to her, relaxing further in his arms as his tongue slipped past her parted lips to dance frantically with hers. The kiss was electrifying, setting her body on fire as she kissed him back. A yearning settled deep in her core. A low moan escaped the back of her throat when Marco deepened the kiss and pushed her back up against the wall, wedging his leg between hers. He lifted her leg, draping it around his hip, and rocked into her.

She tore her mouth from his and stared into his eyes as she lifted her other leg and locked them both around his hips. She breathed in deeply and felt her canine teeth elongate as his scent overwhelmed her. Placing her nose in the crook of his neck, she inhaled again. "You smell like ambrosia." Her voice sounded foreign to her ears.

"You smell the same to me." She nodded as his lips grazed her neck. "It is the way between mates." Tilting her head, she allowed him better access. "Soon, you will sense me even though you cannot see me."

"Intoxicating...I feel so strange...I want to taste...." Amanda closed her eyes and ran her tongue from his collarbone to nip his neck just below his earlobe. "Mmmmm." He tasted as good as he smelled. The urge to bite was almost overwhelming as she felt his cock swell more, and he rocked into her again.

"Keep that up, *il mio amore*, and you won't be leaving my office anytime soon." Her eyes flew open and locked with his. "I would love nothing better than to tear the clothes from your luscious body and pleasure us both until we are both sated...but—"

Amanda dropped her legs and looked away. "Oh, God. What am I doing?" She pushed away from him and took a step toward the door, making an effort to hurriedly tuck in her blouse. "I've got to go...this can't happen again."

Marco gripped her shoulders from behind, stopping her in her tracks, and nipped at her neck. She closed her eyes and shivered. "This *will* happen again, *il mio amore*. Count on it. You are mine. Next time—"

"Marco, there can't be a next time."

"*Next* time, I will lay you over my desk and feast upon that luscious body of yours." She shivered again. "And I will not stop until you've screamed my name at least a dozen times, and we've both had our fill."

CHAPTER FIVE

Amanda lifted a shaky hand to twist the knob on her office door and let it drift closed behind her. Walking past Caroline, she sat behind her desk. Reaching over, she turned on the computer and stared at the bright blue screen without really seeing it.

"Amanda...Amanda...*A m a n d a*...." Caroline narrowed her eyes and rapped her knuckles on the desk. "*Amanda!*"

Amanda sighed heavily, refusing to look at her friend. "What, Caroline?"

"Are you okay?"

"It depends on what your definition of *okay* is."

"Look at me, girlfriend." Amanda shook her head. "Amanda, *look* at me."

Amanda's eyes met Caroline's, and Caroline sucked in a shocked breath. "Wha...what's with your eyes?"

Amanda shrugged and looked away again. "Maybe...." She swallowed hard as a tear slid down her cheek. "Maybe it would be...safer...for you to stay away from me from now on."

"Safer?" Caroline struck the desk with her fist. Amanda didn't even flinch. "Oh, no, you don't, girlfriend. You're not shutting me out now. We share everything, remember?"

As teenagers, Caroline had always managed to worm information out of her friends. Amanda had always thought that Caroline's persistent manner was amusing—until now. Now Caroline's prying could put her in danger, and Amanda wanted no part of it. "Not this."

"Especially this."

"I said, *no!*" Amanda turned her head and glared at her friend. Her eyes turned from glowing amber to a bright red, and her voice dropped an octave as she spoke. "Get the fuck away from me. You're playing with fire, and even *I* don't know what I'm capable of."

Caroline's hands visibly shook as she gripped the arms of the chair, but she shook her head and stood her ground. "No."

Amanda lifted an eyebrow. "No?"

"No," she repeated. "We've been best friends since grade school. We've been through sharing our thoughts on our first dates, first kisses, breakups, letdowns, and everything in between. Something has happened to you. I'm not blind. I can see that, but...I'm here for you, girlfriend. You can tell me anything. *Nothing* you can say will make me leave your side."

Amanda smiled without humor, revealing her larger canines. "Do you want to take bets on that?"

Caroline swallowed hard, then nodded nervously. "You bet." She crossed her heart with her index finger. "I'm here for you."

Amanda sat back in her chair and crossed her arms

over her chest regarding Caroline. "You're either very brave or very…*stupid*."

Caroline's mouth gaped. *"Hey!"*

Amanda sighed heavily, then spoke. *"Vorrei farvi capire. Io non sono sicuro di essere in giro. Andate, per favore, Caroline."*

Caroline cocked her head to the side, confused. "Are you speaking Italian?"

Amanda nodded. *"Sì."*

Caroline bit her thumbnail in a nervous gesture as she studied her friend again. Almost hesitantly, she asked, "But you don't speak Italian, do you?"

"Stop biting your nails." Caroline's face flushed as she jerked her thumbnail from between her teeth. "Thank you. To answer your question, not until today, no."

"Okay, you speak Italian now too…. Interesting…." she said absently, then looked back into Amanda's eyes. "What did you just tell me."

"I begged you to leave me. I'm not safe to be around anymore."

Caroline frowned. "That's just plain nonsense, and you know it." Sitting back in her chair, she appeared to ponder their conversation, then smiled in a teasing manner. "I was joking earlier about the whole vampire thing, but maybe — "

"I'm not a vampire, Caroline," Amanda said impatiently.

"No, no, hear me out." Amanda shook her head, and Caroline charged on. "Your eyes just turned the wickedest shade of red, and those teeth…." She brought her hands up to cover her neck.

Amanda rolled her eyes. "You've been watching too

many late-night horror shows."

She giggled. "Maybe so, but you've got to admit—"

"You'll never get me to admit to being a vampire because I'm not."

"Okay, missy, if you're not a vampire, then what has you acting so strange?"

Amanda bit her bottom lip. "The truth is about as farfetched as your vampire theory. I'm still trying to process the information, and it happened to me."

Caroline shrugged. "I think I just proved to you that I'm not going anywhere until you spill, so...."

"Wolf," Amanda whispered.

Caroline did a double-take and blinked in confusion. "Did you just say 'wolf'?"

Amanda nodded, then watched the transformation from disbelief to humor cross Caroline's features.

Caroline laughed out loud. "You can believe you're a wolf over a vampire?" Her shoulders shook in her laughter. "There is no such thing as a werewolf."

Amanda cocked an eyebrow and smirked at her friend. "You can believe in vampires but not werewolves?"

"Sure, everyone knows that werewolves are a figment of someone's overactive imagination."

"*Oh, mio signore. Dammi la forza.*" Caroline raised an eyebrow in question, so Amanda filled her in. "I just asked God for strength."

Caroline put up her hands. "Okay, okay, so what makes you *think* you're a wolf?"

"For your information, I don't want to *think* that. Geez, Caroline. You act like all this is some huge joke that I'm playing on you."

"I'm sorry, Mandy. I didn't mean to hurt your feelings."

Amanda gave her a small smile. "You haven't called me Mandy since we turned thirteen and thought nicknames were too childish." The smile faded.

"So, sue me." Caroline regarded Amanda's pensive expression, and when she didn't continue, she said, "Nice try. You're avoiding the question."

Amanda looked away again, then shrugged. "It's just all starting to make sense now."

"Amanda, *look* at me." Their eyes met, then Caroline smiled. "Your eyes, they're blue again. Whatever this is, it is obviously triggered by your emotions. Please explain what seems to be making sense to you now so I can understand too."

Amanda splayed her hands. "Everything…my life in general."

"Your life?"

"Yeah, I mean, things haven't been right since we were kids."

"From what I can remember, we seemed to have a pretty normal childhood." Amanda shook her head. "And your parents seemed pretty normal too. I don't remember any wolves around your house growing up…and why do you keep shaking your head *no* at me?"

"I found out last year when Mom died that I was adopted."

Caroline's mouth gaped. "Wow, you never said anything about being adopted."

Amanda shrugged. "Mom's funeral didn't seem to be a

good time to say anything, and after that…well…it just didn't really seem that important.

"I held Mom's hand while she was dying, and she told me about the adoption with her last breath. She said I was put in their care for my protection, and she said my biological mom was dead. She also said to take care during a full moon. I had no idea what she meant at the time, but it's starting to make sense now. I was too shocked to ask any questions, and once she told me everything, she seemed to be at peace and slipped away."

Caroline shook her head. "You're reading more into this than there is. Just because she told you to take care during a full moon doesn't mean that she knew you'd turn into a werewolf. She was sick and could have been delusional. Did you think about that?"

"Of course I did. That's why I've never said anything about it before now. But now…I think there might have been some truth to her words."

"Is all you're basing this on the confession of a dying woman who was, as we both know, terminally ill and quite possibly hallucinating?"

Amanda shook her head, then got up to pace. "No, that's only part of it." She stopped at the bookshelves and picked up a small wolf statue, running her finger down the intricate detail. She looked up and studied the other wolf items lining the shelves.

"You're killing me!" Caroline blurted abruptly.

Placing the statue carefully back onto the shelf, she turned back to her friend. "Sorry, these things…." She waved her hand toward the shelves. "Distracted me. I feel as though

I've seen them before. Held them in my hands…."

"They're just knick-knacks."

Amanda picked up the statue again, then handed it to Caroline. "I thought so, too, at first. Take a good look." Caroline turned the statue over in her hands, then looked back up at Amanda. "It's not a cheap trinket solely for decoration. On closer inspection, it is quite old."

Caroline turned the statue over in her hands and looked up at Amanda. "I see what you mean. Did you see the date on the bottom?" Amanda nodded. "It says 1713. If that's real, this thing is priceless."

"That was my thought, too."

Caroline rose from the chair and placed the statue back on the shelf. She reached for an old wooden jewelry box, picked it up, and turned it over in her hands.

Amanda's eyes widened when she saw the carving on the lid. The snarling wolf matched Marco's pinkie ring.

Caroline caught her breath. "Look, Amanda, there's an inscription on the bottom."

"What does it say?" Amanda asked as she reached for the box.

"I don't know. It's in Italian, but it's dated 1713 like the statue."

È scritto che nell'anno del nostro Signore mille novecento ottantotto un bambino è nato per la nostra specie. Lei è un lupo, cresciuto in innocenza per la sua protezione e la nostra. Con la luce della luna piena, dopo la marcatura del venticinquesimo anno della sua nascita, si salirà di assumere il suo giusto posto sul trono come la nostra regina e compagno al nostro re. Noi, i Lucianadonates,

sarà dotato di un erede, un bambino destinato a governare da parte di padre. Insieme, padre e figlio saranno invincibili e noi come razza regneranno per l'eternità. Attenzione, ci sono quelli in opposizione messa in atto per fermarla. Ella deve perseverare, se non siamo condannati.
    —Nicolai Lucianadontes 1713

    Caroline placed the box in her hands. "Can you read it?" Caroline asked.

    Amanda squinted her eyes. "I'll try. The print is so small." She ran her fingers over the engraving. "It says, 'It is written that in the year of our Lord nineteen hundred and eighty-eight a child will be born to our kind. She is a wolf, raised in innocence for her protection and ours. By the light of the full moon, following the marking of the twenty-fifth year of her birth, she will rise to assume her rightful place on the throne as our queen and mate to our king. We, the Lucianadonates, will be gifted with an heir, a child destined to rule by their father's side. Together father and son will be invincible, and we, as a race, will rule for eternity. Beware, there are those in opposition set in place to stop her. She must persevere. If not, we are doomed. —Nicolai Lucianadonates 1713.'"

    Amanda looked up from the box, and Caroline was staring at her.

    "Amanda, you were born in 1988." Amanda looked at the box again. "You just had your twenty-fifth birthday too." Amanda bit her lip and nodded. "The full moon is next weekend."

    "Caroline—"

"Well, it is!"

Amanda placed the jewelry box back on the shelf. "I thought you didn't believe that I was a wolf."

"Well…uh…." Amanda raised an eyebrow. "I guess you might be right."

"Hmmm…somehow, that doesn't really make me feel any better." She walked over to her office chair and plopped down. "What am I going to do?"

CHAPTER SIX

Amanda turned the lock and set the deadbolt, then threw her purse and keys on the table next to the door. It had been a very long day. She and Caroline had brainstormed most of the afternoon and still didn't have any definitive answers. Now, all she wanted was to take a hot bath and go to bed.

She hadn't seen Marco again around the office, which she figured was probably a good thing because she needed time. Today was just too much, too soon.

The scent of lavender permeated the air when she poured the bath salts into the steaming water. She smiled. This was her favorite way to relax and hopefully forget the stress-filled day she'd just had.

One of the best perks of the apartment was the huge spa tub in the master bath. Bending over the jetted tub, she lit the candles on the tile ledges, setting the room off in a soft glow. With any luck, she'd be able to forget her troubles—at least for a short while.

She grabbed a hair clip off the counter and clipped her waist-length black hair on top of her head as she gingerly stepped into the water, lowering herself, then reclining back until the hot water bubbled gently at her breasts and neck.

Amanda closed her eyes, letting out a long contented sigh. The slight noise from the bubbling water and the pulsating current soothed her. As her body relaxed, she felt herself drift off.

A vision of Marco swam before her half-open eyelids. He stood next to the tub, gazing down at her. His shirt hung open, leaving his chest bare. She watched the muscles contract as he placed his hands on his hips. The movement drew her gaze downward over his rippling abs to the line of hair that started at his navel and disappeared into his pants. He wore the jeans low on his hips, the snap and zipper open, barely concealing his swelling cock. He was everything she had imagined and more—perfect. The corners of her mouth turned up in a lazy smile. She sighed again as she watched him free his cock and fist it, gently stroking it as he continued to watch her. She had no thoughts to cover herself; he was, after all, just a dream.

"Do you like what you see, *il mio amore*?"

She licked her lips as his jeans slid down his legs, pooling at his feet. "Mmmm."

"You are a gift from the gods, bellissimi." He stepped over the side of the tub. "May I join you?"

As his leg brushed hers, her eyes flew wide open—this was no dream. She sat up so fast that water sloshed onto the floor. "What the hell?" She stood up and reached for the towel. "How in the hell did you even get in here?" Marco snatched up the towel and held it out of her reach. "You've got to be fucking kidding me!" Amanda curled her lip back in a snarl. "Give me the towel, Marco."

He flashed her a brilliantly white smile as he ran his fingers lightly down the side of her heaving breast. "No, I prefer you without it."

Amanda slapped his hand away. "You have no right to touch me. Keep your fucking hands to yourself and give me the towel."

Marco shook his head, undaunted, reaching for her breast again. "I have every right, *il mio amore*. We are mates."

"Not if I kill you first," she said as her fist connected with his jaw. Marco barely flinched, but she could see the mark turn red to purple and then fade in less than a second. She took a shocked step back when he winked at her and continued his pursuit.

"You see? I told you this morning that you cannot physically harm me."

Dodging his hand, she backed into the corner. "Get out. Leave. I don't want you here. I don't want *you*."

Marco took a step toward her, cupping her cheek with his hand, tilting her chin up to gaze into her eyes. "Ah, but you *will*, *l'amore*, you will." She jerked her chin away from his grasp, glaring back into his eyes. "I love your spirit, my little *alfa lupo*. You and I are well matched."

Growling deep, Amanda shoved Marco away from her, sloshing more water out of the tub. "And you, sir, are delusional," she huffed as she stepped out of the tub. "So...." She fisted her hands as she searched for words in her anger. "...so fucking full of yourself."

Marco stepped out of the tub, blocking her exit and holding the towel tauntingly out of her reach.

Putting out her hand, she said, "Give it to me."

He shook his head, laughing softly. "No."

"Oh, for Christ's sake," Amanda said under her breath, eyeing the towel. Setting her jaw, her eyes cut to his. He raised an eyebrow in challenge. Her words were low and deliberate. "Give. Me. The. Fucking. Towel."

He laughed harder. "No, *tesoro,* I will not. If you want the towel, you will have to *take* it from me."

Amanda had never met anyone more infuriating in her life. And he expected her just to accept everything he said as gospel and bow down to his every whim? Not fucking likely. *Two can play at this game,* she thought. As she dodged to the left, he shifted the towel to his other hand. "Asshole," she growled, lunging in the other direction as he switched hands again.

"You'll have to do better than that, *tesoro,* if you wish to shield yourself from me." His eyes traveled the length of her body, darkening with need. He inhaled deeply, taking in her scent. "You are the most beautiful creature I've ever seen, *l'amore,* and I have lived a great many years."

Amanda felt his gaze like a physical caress, and her body responded to his words…they consumed her against her will. She felt her nipples pebble and swallowed hard. "So you say, Marco. For all I know, your words are just that—words." Her heart rate picked up as she glanced around the room for a quick exit. She saw none. *Distract him, dummy.* Marco stared into her eyes as if reading her thoughts and smirked. She felt the panic building…she had to at least try, so she continued, "A speech you put together nicely so that you think I'll just bow down and fall into your bed." Her chin rose a notch. "That's not going to happen."

"You forget that I can read your thoughts. *Your* own body betrays *your* words." Marco inhaled again, a lazy grin forming at the corners of his mouth, his cock thickening by the second. "I can smell your arousal, *l'amore*. It calls to my wolf, and he grows impatient for his mate." He fisted his cock with his free hand, stroking slowly and deliberately as she watched. A pearl of cum formed at the tip. She licked her lips, then he continued. "As for me, the man, I enjoy your games. When I bury my cock deep inside of you...." She shook her head no. " —and I will, you can be assured of that—it will be all the sweeter for both of us."

"You would force yourself on me?"

"Never."

She swallowed hard, taking a small step back in an effort to put some distance between them. "Well then, what do you call this?"

"Persuasion."

"It feels more like coercion to me."

He lowered his arm, and her eyes caught the movement. "Finally," she said triumphantly. Taking Marco off guard, she made a dodge for the towel. Her foot slipped in the water pooled on the floor, sending her headlong, full force into Marco. He dropped the towel as he wrapped his arms around her to break her fall. Her nose was buried in the crook of his neck as he embraced her.

"Careful, *l'amore*. I do not want to see you hurt."

Amanda breathed in his scent. Need suddenly coiled in the pit of her belly, and her body was on fire. "Marco," she breathed his name out as she buried her nose deeper. He rocked his hips, pressing his hard cock into her flesh. She moaned and licked the vein in his neck to the base of his ear. Her canines dropped as she scraped her teeth over his vein, pricking the skin. Suckling the hurt, her tongue lapping at the small bead of blood, the taste left her giddy.

Marco growled low, tightening his grip and rocking his hips again. "*Vacci, amore*...slowly, or I won't be able to be gentle with you. Your wolf is calling to her mate, and *he* is not patient. *He* wants her to submit to him."

Amanda reached between them, stroking his cock with one hand. The other she slipped between her own legs to rub over her sensitive clit. His scent was controlling her now, driving her on to do things she normally did in private. Slipping two fingers inside her pussy, she plunged them in and out in rhythm to her other hand, stroking his cock. His cock was hot to her touch, a combination of rock hard and velvet smooth, and slid easily in her grip. Her fingers moved faster in her pussy as she imagined his cock plunging into her. She felt her juices run down her legs as the ache grew to nearly unbearable.

Marco held her tightly and moaned, surging his hips in rhythm to her fingers, squeezing the blood-filled crown. As the pre-cum dripped from the tiny eye over her hand, his cock became slick, and her hand moved faster.

"I feel so strange," she panted. "I need...." Her body bucked as her release took her.

Marco scooped her up in his arms and carried her into the bedroom, placing her gently onto the bed. He knelt between her legs, and their eyes met.

He was the most beautiful thing she had ever seen. Amanda watched the muscles ripple as he adjusted her hips on the bed. His body was flawless. Every muscle in his chest and abs was sculpted to perfection, without an ounce of fat. She licked her lips as she stared at his cock. It was thick and stood out from his body proudly, the purple crown engorged, seeping pre-cum. Their eyes met again.

"Pleasure yourself as you did a moment ago." His voice came out in a low growl. "I want to watch your fingers disappear into your heat."

She bit her bottom lip and moved her fingers over her pussy again and watched Marco's reaction as she inserted three fingers and plunged them deep inside. She was wet for him and ached to have him fill her.

He grabbed his cock and stroked it as he watched her pleasure herself.

She spread her legs wider, allowing him to see more of her. When she saw a pearl of cum drip from the tip of his cock, her fingers picked up the pace and continued to spear in and out of her pussy as he watched, brushing the hardened nub at the juncture each time she rocked her hips. She had never done that in front of anyone before, and his watching made it seem erotic. She caught her breath again as another climax took her. She felt his gaze on her pussy and knew he watched as she pulsated around her fingers.

Marco let go of his cock, then pulled her fingers from her pussy and took them into his mouth, sucking each digit clean.

The feel of him sucking her fingers had her hips coming off the bed with a deeper, raw need. "Please...." she begged.

"My wolf has had a taste of you, and *he* wants to fuck his mate.... *He* will not allow me to be gentle."

Amanda's eyes glowed red as she spoke. "I need you," she growled, her fangs extended.

Marco poised his cock at her entrance, a trickle of sweat trailing down his back as he tried to restrain his wolf. As she wrapped her legs around his hips, the head of his cock entered her pussy, and he was lost. In one thrust, he buried himself deep within her heat. She had him so hard that it was all he could do to keep from coming on the first plunge. Amanda whimpered and rocked her hips up to meet his. He withdrew his cock only to dive in again and again. Her body perfectly timed with his bowing up off the bed, taking all he could give her as he drove on. Her feet let go, her body trembling, as his pace quickened more, and he drove harder and faster until he felt her let go. He came hard, his own body shaking as her pussy milked his cock. Marco collapsed on top of her, and both were out within seconds.

CHAPTER SEVEN

Beep. Beep. Beep. Beep.

Peeling an eye open, Amanda looked at the time, 5:30 a.m., then reached over and pushed the *off* button. She rolled over onto her back and stared at the ceiling, wondering how much of last night was real and how much her overactive imagination had fabricated. Turning her head, she placed her palm on the cold sheets. "Of course, he'd be gone. What else did you expect?" she grumbled to herself.

I haven't gone anywhere. And it was all real. I figured I'd add that part in to ease your mind.

Amanda furrowed her brow, raising up on her elbows to look around the room in confusion. "Marco?"

Sì?

She threw the covers back, easing her legs over the side of the bed. Reaching for her robe, she wrapped it around her to stave off the chill in the room. Amanda stood, turning a slow circle as she looked around her darkened bedroom. "If you're here, where are you?" She bent down and looked beneath the bed, then stood, her eyes searching the dark corners of the room. "Okay, okay, I believe you that we're wolves. And after

last night…I guess I can believe the mate part, too. But….”
Throwing open the closet door, she searched through the rack
of clothes that Marco might be hiding behind.

But?

She turned around and faced the bed, placed her hands
on her hips, and huffed, “Girls don’t like it when guys just
disappear on them in the morning. It makes them feel cheap
and used. Where the hell are you? Do you sport some powers
that I’m not aware of—like invisibility?”

She heard him laugh. *You are none of those things, l’amore,
and yes, we both have powers that you will learn, but no, I cannot
make myself invisible.*

Amanda stamped her foot in frustration. “You are
dancing around my questions, giving me answers but not
answering a damn thing. Where are you?”

Marco opened the bedroom door, stepping inside with
a spatula in his hand, his body bare to her gaze. “I answered
your questions, *tesoro*. We cannot make ourselves invisible.”

He looks good enough to eat danced through her mind.
Marco flashed her a smile.

“Where were you?”

He held up the spatula. “In the kitchen.”

She stared at the spatula in disbelief. “You mean you’re
telling me you’ve been here all along, and you cook?”

“*Sì*…how do you like your eggs?”

Amanda shrugged. “I don’t normally eat breakfast.
In fact, I’m amazed that you even found any eggs in the
refrigerator in the first place.”

“I didn’t. I had to go to my apartment and get them.”
He backed out of the doorway. “*Un momento per favore*. The

steak is getting cold."

Amanda stood there dumbfounded for a few seconds before his words registered, and her stomach growled. She followed in his wake. "Wait a minute, what apartment?" The smells coming from the kitchen had her mouth-watering. "And did you just say you cooked steak?"

"*Sì*, nothing but the best for my beautiful mate," he said as he scrambled the eggs in the pan. "I hope you like your eggs scrambled. It is the fastest way to cook them, and I, for one, am hungry." He looked over at her and winked. "I worked up an appetite last night and figured you did as well."

She felt the blush all the way down to her toes. She shook her head and leaned her hip against the counter. "We need to talk."

He laughed softly. "Yes, we do, and we will...over breakfast." He turned the stove off. "Do you mind setting the table so we can eat?"

Amanda grabbed the plates and utensils, setting a place for two. Marco filled the plates and poured two cups of coffee. He came up behind her, placed his hand on her shoulder, and brushed a kiss on her cheek as he pulled out her chair. "Please be seated."

She sat and smiled up at him. "You know that's really not necessary. Most men don't do that."

He sat across from her. "I grew up in an era where we cherished our women, as I do you. I will continue to treat you with the respect you deserve."

Amanda picked up her utensils and nodded at his comment. "Thank you." She cut into her steak. It was very rare, as she seemed to like it now. Cutting a small piece, she placed it in her mouth and chewed with a smile of contentment. "Mmmm…this is excellent." She licked a little juice from the corner of her mouth and caught Marco staring at her. His fork was halfway to his mouth, and his eyes had darkened. She smiled at his expression, then looked down at herself. "What…? Did I drop some on myself?"

Marco choked out the word "no" and adjusted himself in the chair, then cleared his throat. "No," he said again, a little louder. "Keep that up, and we'll wind up back in your room instead of going into the office today."

She tilted her head, her smile broadening as he readjusted himself in the chair. "What did I do?" She popped another piece of steak into her mouth as she attempted to look over the table.

He dropped his napkin in his lap. The corners of his mouth turned up in a smile. "You know very well what I'm referring to." He placed the piece of steak into his mouth and chewed.

Winking at him, she popped another piece of steak into her mouth. She placed her fork back onto her plate as she sat back in her chair, and swallowed the last bite. "Marco, we really do need to talk."

He nodded, putting his fork down as well. "I know."

She toyed with her napkin as she spoke, "Some things…you said last night…and before." She took in a deep breath, letting it out in a whoosh. "They don't really make much sense."

"I know you have questions."

She nodded. "I do." Amanda placed the napkin back

onto the table. "I know you said we have…powers…." Marco nodded. "But I need to know how you got into my apartment."

He laughed softly. "I didn't use any special 'power' to get into your apartment, *l'amore*."

Amanda threw up her hands. "How did you do it then? Do I need to somehow beef up my security, complain to management, what?"

"I am management."

She did a double-take. "What?"

"I had this building built, and I sometimes occupy the unit next door. It is much larger than this one. I have investments such as this one all over Chicago."

"O-k-a-y," she dragged out the word. "That still doesn't explain how you got through a locked and bolted door."

"I didn't." He rose from his chair and walked behind hers. "Let me show you." She stood next to him. "Would you like to see my apartment?"

Her eyes devoured his unclad body as she shook her head. "I'm not dressed yet, and you're not dressed at all. If someone were to see us in the hallway—"

"They won't."

"But they might."

"Come, Amanda, come with me."

"All right." She placed her coffee cup down on the table and left the kitchen.

Marco laughed. "Where are you going?"

Amanda spun around. "*Duh*, to your apartment."

He shook his head, motioning her back into the kitchen. "No, this way."

"What, you can walk through walls now?"

"Something like that."

"I was joking."

Marco kissed her on the cheek, taking her hand. "I know you were. However, I wasn't." He opened the pantry door and ran his fingers above the top shelf. The wall silently slid back and away, opening into another room.

Amanda blinked in astonishment. "You had a secret entrance into my apartment?"

"This apartment was never meant to be rented to anyone but my future mate. It was designed specifically for you, *l'amore*."

"So this is how...Marco, this is *wrong* on so many levels."

"You did not know me, and according to the prophecy, I had to wait before I revealed myself to you. In the meantime, I had to be able to protect you."

She looked around his apartment. "Well, that explains a few things." She threw out her hands and shrugged. "What now?"

"I understand you're upset."

She looked away and shrugged again. "I'll get over it." She ran her fingers across the marble countertops and gazed into the grand living area. *Marco has excellent taste*, she thought. *I wish....*

"Thank you," he said as he approached the counter and stood next to her.

She glanced up into his eyes. "What are you thanking me for?"

"Your thoughts...for not being angry with me."

Amanda tilted her head. "How do you do that,

anyway?"

He shrugged. "If you concentrate hard enough, you can do it too." Marco lifted her chin and placed a soft kiss on her lips. *But with me, you won't necessarily need to concentrate.*

She jabbed her index finger into his chest. "That's what I'm talking about. How do you talk inside my head like that?"

"We are mates. We have a connection." He gazed into her eyes. *Open your mind, Amanda, and speak to me with your mind. You have tasted my blood, so I know you can do this.*

"Okay."

Marco placed his finger over her lips. *With your mind, l'amore.*

This is never going to work, Marco.

He let out a bark of laughter. "It just did."

She raised an eyebrow. "Okay, what did I say?"

You said that this would never work. Although I do beg to differ with you. We are making it work.

Okay, I will repeat an earlier question. Amanda shrugged again as she sighed. *What now?*

"You do not leave my side until after the ceremony on Friday."

CHAPTER EIGHT

Marco whipped his Aston Martin DBS to a stop in front of the Glasko building. He glanced at Amanda's rigid profile… she hadn't uttered a word the entire drive there. Amanda had voiced her complaints several times while in his apartment about his insisting that she "not leave his side." Her complaints so far had fallen on deaf ears—Marco hadn't swayed an inch.

She glared at Marco as he made his way around the car and opened her door for her, then handed his key to the valet attendant.

"Come on, Amanda, the attendant is waiting."

"Is this really necessary, Marco?" Amanda huffed.

"I told you earlier that it is."

She reluctantly slid out of the car seat and grabbed her purse. "People will talk if they see me walk into the building with you."

Marco closed the car door, waving the attendant on. "Who?"

She shrugged as he ushered her toward the building. "Charlie, Ray, and some of the others."

He held the front door to the building open for her as

she walked past him. "What reason would they have to talk about you?"

Amanda handed her badge to the guard. "Mornin', Ms. Archer."

"Hi, Joe. How's the missus?"

"You're always such a darlin' for askin'. I haven't heard her complainin'. I'll let her know you asked about her."

"You do that. And Joe...tell her I miss seeing her here."

"Yes, ma'am. I'll do that."

Joe scanned Marco's badge. "Good to see you, Mr. De Lucia."

"You too, Joe."

Marco escorted her past the security station. "Well?"

She stopped, forcing him to stop as well. Crossing her arms over her chest, she glared up at him. "If you must know, Charlie overheard Caroline tell me that you insisted I head the job. If I refused the job, Glasko wouldn't get the account. Charlie assumed that I was sleeping with you."

"I see."

"I don't think you do. I *wasn't* sleeping with you. I didn't even *know* you." He nodded. "Now that I have...." She sighed. "I have mixed feelings of guilt."

Amanda saw Charlie approaching them but said nothing to Marco. She figured Charlie was making an attempt to "suck up" to the new boss.

"You have nothing to feel guilty about. The job was yours, regardless." Charlie stopped a few feet from them. "You earned it and were the best employee suited for it. As far as Glasko not getting the account is concerned...that's nonsense. I am the major shareholder in this firm—a somewhat silent partner."

"Charlie is still going to say that you used favoritism in picking me. He thinks he's the best advertising executive that Glasko has."

Marco scowled. "I did review Charlie and Ray's work and found it inferior. In fact, if their work doesn't improve, I will be replacing them soon."

Marco, we have company.

Marco looked behind him and saw Charlie hurry to the elevator across the room. "Did you know he was there?"

Amanda nodded. "Sure did."

"And you didn't stop me. Why?"

She dropped her arms and shrugged. "I thought Charlie was sneaking over here to suck up to 'the new boss.' I had no clue that you were going to say something negative about him while he was listening. Besides, with as much grief as he's put me through…well, let's just say he had that one coming."

Marco shook his head and guided her toward the elevators. "I never really thought of you as being vindictive."

She pushed the button and shrugged again. "You don't really know me…you just think you do."

"I'm usually a good judge of character. You might be pissed at me, but you wouldn't take your anger at me out on others." The doors slid open, and they stepped inside.

As the doors slid closed, Amanda turned back to Marco and replied, "No, I wouldn't. In my own defense, I'm not generally vindictive, no, but Charlie has gotten on my last nerve, and I have to work with these people, Marco. I don't like to be gossiped about."

"If Charlie gives you any more trouble, just let me know."

Amanda rolled her eyes. "I can handle Charlie," she said as she stepped off the elevator and ran into Caroline.

Caroline grabbed Amanda's shoulders to steady her as Amanda stumbled. "Whoa there, girlfriend. Are you okay?"

Amanda glared at Marco as he let out a bark of laughter. "I'll be fine after I kill his ass," Amanda growled.

"Amanda!" Caroline whispered harshly. "He'll hear you."

"Good."

Marco laughed louder.

Caroline raised an eyebrow at Amanda, then flashed Marco a huge grin. "Good morning, Mr. De Lucia."

"Good morning, Ms. Robinson. Nice catch."

Caroline laughed with him. "Er, thanks."

Amanda glared at her. "*Et tu, Brute?*"

Caroline laughed harder. "Quoting Shakespeare now? I am not a traitor." Amanda glared harder. "What...? You've got to admit that *was* funny." Amanda growled low. Caroline stopped laughing and glanced nervously at Marco. "I was just playing...behave before someone hears you."

Amanda glanced at Marco, then shrugged. "Is your reference to that 'someone' being Marco?"

Caroline nodded, then glanced nervously at Marco again. "Marco?" she whispered. "You're on a first name basis with the boss?"

You walked into that one all on your own, l'amore. I'll be in my office. Don't leave this floor.

Amanda pulled her upper lip back in a snarl. *I'll go*

where I damn well please when I please.

Caroline shook Amanda's shoulders again and whispered. "Amanda! Stop snarling. You'll get yourself fired."

Just stay on this floor. That is not a request.

Asshole.

Marco laughed louder as he continued to his office.

Caroline steered Amanda's shoulders toward her office door. "We need to talk."

Caroline closed the office door as Amanda sat down behind her desk and booted the computer, then she sat down across from Amanda. "Do you want to get fired?"

Amanda sat back and regarded Caroline's worried expression. "Marco won't fire me."

Caroline laughed without humor. "If I were your boss and you treated me like that—I'd fire your ass in a heartbeat."

"Gee, thanks for your vote of confidence."

"I'm not trying to be mean or a bitch, girlfriend…I'm just worried about you."

"You don't need to worry about me—I'm fine."

Caroline studied Amanda for a full minute before she spoke again. "Maybe you should take Jeffrey back."

Amanda's eyes widened. "Why?"

"Maybe if you got laid…."

Amanda heard Marco growl and burst out laughing. "That's not going to happen, Caroline, so get that notion right out of your head."

Caroline smiled. "Why not? You could use him like he used you…you know, work out those sexual frustrations that have you so keyed up."

I don't want you talking to her.

I will talk to whomever I damn well please.

No, I'll not allow this to continue. She's putting ideas into your head.

Not allow? You don't really want to go there.

You are mine, Amanda....

Amanda rolled her eyes. *Whatever...this macho crap is getting on my nerves.* He growled low. *She's my best friend, Marco. She's just worried about me.*

You better control her, or I'll have to get rid of her.

I'll have to tell her then.

No.

She can keep a secret.

No.

She already knows I'm a wolf....

Silence.

She'll help me through this....

Fine, but if she proves she can't be trusted....

I know, I know....

Caroline snapped her fingers in front of Amanda's face several times. "Earth to Amanda...hello?"

Amanda shook her head, then focused in on Caroline. "Sorry."

"Where did you go? You zoned out on me." Caroline grinned. "Thinking about my suggestion?"

Amanda heard Marco growl again and nearly choked. "No."

Caroline sat back in her chair and frowned. "Why not? It might do you some good, and I'm positive that Jeffrey wants to come back."

Amanda shook her head and mouthed, "no way."

"You used to brag about how good Jeffrey was in bed."

"It would be a cold day in hell before I allowed Jeffrey to even step foot into my apartment, much less into my bed." Amanda grinned at her friend when she opened her mouth to protest. "Besides, I've had better. Jeffrey might be nice to look at, but he's a very selfish bed partner."

Caroline's eyes widened as she sat forward in her chair again with a smile of anticipation. "Oooh, *better* than Jeffrey. This I've got to hear. You've been holding out on me."

"No, I haven't."

"Yeah, I'm pretty sure that you have. I don't think I'd forget a juicy story. Who is he? What does he look like? Does he have a friend?"

Amanda heard Marco laugh.

"Geez, Caroline, chill, will ya?"

"Oh, come on, Mandy, my sex life is on the outs, and I have to live mine vicariously through you."

"Do you know how pathetic that sounds?"

Caroline shrugged. "So sue me. What I need to hear is that there is still hope for some good times for a single lady out there while I'm still young enough to enjoy it. Please tell me he has a friend."

"I…I don't know if he has any single friends."

Do you?

"P-l-e-a-s-e."

Do I what?

Oh, come on, Marco, I know you've been listening. She's my best friend.

It might be a way to keep an eye on her to make sure she

doesn't share our secret. I'll see what I can do.

Amanda smiled. *Thank you.*

"You're smiling. Does that mean you thought of someone, and he does have a friend?"

"I don't know yet, girlfriend, but I'll let you know as soon as I do."

"You're the best, Mandy. Now...." Caroline sat forward in her chair, crossing her arms over the desk. "I'm all ears. I want to know *everything*—who this mystery man is—how he makes you howl—*everything*."

Amanda smirked. "Caroline."

I'm listening too. I want to hear how I make you howl.

Amanda's eyes widened. "*Stop.*"

"What? We both already know you're a wolf." Caroline's grin grew. "I'm sure howling comes with the territory."

Yes, it does come with the territory, l'amore. Howl for me.

Amanda felt his words travel through her, triggering a need deep in the depths of her core. She shivered and felt her panties grow wet.

I can sense how you're feeling. Come to me, and we'll pick up where we left off last night. I can spread you across my desk and taste you.

Amanda crossed her legs and shifted in the chair. The need grew instead of easing, increasing her frustration. "Stop it! You're both starting to confuse me," she whined to both.

Amanda growled when she heard Marco laugh.

Marco, I will make you pay for this.

He laughed harder. *That sounds like a challenge. You should know better than to challenge an alfa. Come to me now, l'amore.*

"Both?" Caroline sat up straight, then glanced around the room. "Why are you growling? Who else is in the room?"

Swallowing hard, Amanda closed her eyes, then took a deep quivering breath. She felt compelled to go to Marco's office and had to grip the arms of her chair with her fingernails to keep from complying with the demand. Her forehead and upper lip beaded with a light sheen of sweat with the strain. Feeling her control building, she opened her eyes, and Caroline was staring at her wide-eyed.

I, too, am an alfa, and I will come to your office when I damn well please.

"Amanda, you're making me nervous. Your eyes have changed, and you seem to be speaking to someone I can't see. What's going on?"

You learn quickly, la mia piccola Alfa Lupo.

She ignored Marco. "I'm sorry, Caroline. I'm still struggling with all this myself. There is no one else in the room with us. You can relax. I will not harm you."

Caroline let out a harried breath. "Seriously?" She shook her head and sat back in her chair, crossing one leg over the other. "Mandy, we've been friends forever. Will you please stop acting like I'm afraid of you? Geez, we grew up together, for Christ's sake. You're my best friend. I *know* you're not going to hurt me. I just thought someone else was in the room who might. So stop apologizing."

"Okay."

Caroline drummed her fingers on the arm of the chair and narrowed her eyes. "Now, we were in the process of you telling me something very juicy when you spaced out on me again."

"I'm sor—" Caroline raised an eyebrow, and Amanda smiled. "I was going to apologize again, wasn't I?" Caroline nodded. "It all started with the dream I told you about."

Caroline smirked. "I'm not referring to a dream. I'm referring to the real thing."

Amanda shrugged. "It was as real as it gets, girlfriend."

"But…you said it was a dream."

"I thought it was at first." Amanda bit her bottom lip. "I have a lot to tell you, but you have to have an open mind and have to promise me that you won't tell a soul. It could cost us both our jobs if you do."

Caroline held up her hand. "Scout's honor."

Amanda raised an eyebrow. "You were never a Girl Scout, Caroline."

Caroline waved off her hand. "That's just an expression, girlfriend." She made the sign of a cross over her heart with her index finger. "Cross my heart. I won't breathe a word of what you tell me to another soul."

"I'm going to hold you to it." Caroline nodded, then Amanda pointed to the bookcase. "Do you remember the jewelry box from yesterday?"

Caroline looked at the shelf, then back to Amanda. "The one with the old inscription on it?" Amanda nodded. "Yeah, sure. What about it?"

"It's all true."

"What?"

"The prophecy on the box—all of it."

"I was afraid of that." Caroline sat back and drummed her fingers on the arm of the chair again in thought, then looked up at Amanda. "What does that have to do with your dream?"

"Well…it wasn't a dream. It happened."

"Oh, my God! How?"

"It was all part of the prophecy. Marco really hasn't explained it, but I'm assuming it is a ceremony to awaken my inner wolf."

It is.

Caroline caught her breath, staring at Amanda, dumbfounded. "Marco…you mean our new boss? Mr. Dreamy?"

Mr. Dreamy?

That's what Caroline and Stacey call you…don't let it go to your head.

"Uh, yeah. That would be him."

Caroline giggled. "So that's why you're calling him by his first name instead of Mr. De Lucia. You're sleeping with the *boss*."

"Caroline! Keep your voice down."

"Oh, sorry. Oh my God, I can't believe it. No wonder you don't want Jeffrey back." Caroline's eyes widened. "That means he's—"

"Yeah, he's like me, or I'm like him. I don't know what to think anymore."

"Is, uh, he the guy the prophecy refers to?" She snapped her fingers a few times as she thought back. "What were the words on the box? It said something about a king and…." Her eyes met Amanda's. "He's your mate."

Marco laughed. *Smart girl. She catches on fast. You should take lessons.*

Button it, Marco. Sarcasm isn't helping your cause.

"He has told me this on several occasions, yes. I'm…I don't know…. My feelings are torn because I like to make my own decisions, and I'm having a difficult time being *told* what I am and am not going to do…or who to love. I guess it's put me in a sour mood."

"Sweetie, you're still entitled to make your own decisions, but we're talking *fate* here."

Amanda looked away. "Yeah, a word that takes all the control for my future away from me."

"You can't look at it that way."

"How else am I supposed to see it? *He* is an alfa. *He* demands control. And me?" She shook her head. "I don't follow orders very well—at least when it concerns my personal life. We're like oil and vinegar."

Caroline winced. "I do hear what you're sayin', baby girl…but in all honesty, if God chose to saddle me with a package like that for the rest of my life, I'd be hitting my knees and thanking him every night for my blessings—wolf or no."

Amanda rolled her eyes. "Caroline—"

"I'm not kidding you, baby girl. God has granted you with a gift. Any single girl out there, and I bet a lot of married ones too, would sell their soul to have a problem such as yours. Look at the total package. My God, the man is sex on a stick and then some. I think we need to get your eyes and hormones checked." Caroline shrugged, grinning devilishly when Amanda opened her mouth to protest. "They say opposites attract."

"I never said I wasn't attracted to the man. As you said, I'd have to be blind not to be. The man can make my insides melt with just a look. To be held in his arms...." Amanda hugged herself and smiled. "...it feels like heaven. When I'm in his arms and breathe in his scent...well, it has a way of making me forget that I was pissed off with him in the first place." Caroline's grin grew. "When I'm alone with the man for more than two minutes, all I want to do is rip our clothes off and have my wicked way with him." Caroline giggled. "There are reasons women fantasize about a man like that." Then Amanda sighed. "Then he opens his mouth and starts ordering me around and ruins the fantasy."

Caroline gave her a mock pout. "Oh, boo."

Amanda sat back in her chair and regarded her friend again. "I know you don't understand my issue, but—"

"Oh, I understand very well," Caroline cut in. "No relationship is perfect, girlfriend. There is give and take on both sides. Most times, it seems like a good relationship is more give than take. Mama always said that if there is love, it'll all work itself out."

"I never said I loved him."

"Who are you trying to fool, me or yourself?"

"What?"

"You *are* in love with the man."

"Caroline Robinson, where do you come up with shit like that?"

"I'm not talking 'shit,' and you know it. Sometimes it takes a best friend to point out the obvious to you. You *are* in love with the man. You're just too stubborn to admit it, even to yourself."

I'm liking this girl more and more.

Amanda slapped her hand on the desk in frustration.

"You are delusional. Didn't you just hear a word I've said?"

Caroline nodded. "Yes, every word."

"And?"

"And I'm gonna quote my mama, 'Don't sweat the small stuff.'"

"I don't think losing my free will and independence is 'small stuff.'"

Caroline stood, then walked over to the bookshelf and picked up the jewelry box. She held it up in reference. "I believe in destiny. *He* is *your* destiny." She placed the box back on the shelf. Amanda opened her mouth to speak, and Caroline held up her hand. "No, let me finish." She turned back to Amanda and leaned against the desk. "Most of us only get one real shot at happiness. And I, for one, have never found anyone...." A tear slid down her cheek. "Who makes me feel a fraction of what you just described to me. So what if he's a little bossy?" She shrugged, then swiped away the tear. "What man isn't? No one is perfect—even you, girlfriend. You can be a bit 'bossy' yourself, and he puts up with *you* with no complaints, doesn't he?"

Amanda sat back and thought about what Caroline said. "Yes," she said under her breath.

"You see? Things aren't really as dismal as your mind is fabricating. Give the guy some slack and let yourself feel. You might surprise yourself."

CHAPTER NINE

Amanda stood outside Marco's door and raised her hand to knock. She had just spent the last couple of hours in her office after Caroline left, stewing over their conversation. It was time to confront Marco. If she didn't, she'd never get any work done because she couldn't think of anything else.

"Come in, *l'amore*." Amanda opened the door and stepped inside, closing it softly behind her. "There is no need for you to knock, *tesoro*. You are always welcome in my office."

Marco rose from his desk to greet her and kissed her on the cheek before she sat down across from his desk. He sat back down behind his desk and regarded her before he spoke. He felt her unease, and she looked nervous. "Your mind has been in turmoil since Caroline left your office."

Amanda nodded. "Yes, yes, it has."

"And?"

"I've given a lot of consideration to the conversation between me and Caroline."

"Oh?"

Amanda looked away. "She's right."

"Hmmm, I see you're still conflicted."

She took in a deep breath and let it out, then looked into his eyes. "I am." She swallowed hard. "I don't easily admit when I am wrong."

"And what exactly are you admitting that you are *wrong* about?"

"*You. Us.* I never really gave you a chance, and I am sorry for that. You just came on so strong, taking me off guard, that it put me on the defensive. I've never been blindsided like that before. I'm usually the one in control, and I've always liked it that way. And if the truth be known and had we been introduced by friends or had met by chance, it would have probably been me pursuing you, not the other way around. You would have probably been the one running in the other direction."

Marco smiled. "Never."

Amanda smiled in return. "Never say never."

"To be chased so ardently by one as fair as you—" His smile grew as he sat back in his chair. "A man dreams of such things happening."

She laughed softly. "You speak so old-fashioned."

"I *am* old, by your standards anyway." He sat forward in his chair and clasped his hands together on top of his desk. "I have changed my mind about your friend Caroline. She is loyal to you."

Amanda nodded. "Yes, almost to a fault."

"Loyalty is an admirable trait and something to cherish. She may be a little inane at times, but she is loyal. My enforcer, Rafael, has not found a mate, and they may find each other to their mutual liking. I will introduce them."

Amanda shook her head. "Marco, you don't really

have to do that."

"But I do. She has helped my cause and may be good for Rafael's disposition."

"Marco—"

"Do not worry, my pet. I will not force either of them. I will just arrange the meeting, and if it's meant to be, it will."

"My pet? Marco, I'm not an animal—" He winked at her, and she frowned. "Don't call me that."

"It was meant as an endearment, not an insult."

"I'm aware of that, but it does remind me that I'm not entirely human."

He tilted his head. "You're not human at all, Amanda, *tu sei il lupo.*"

"I know I'm a wolf. You keep reminding me of that... wait...did you just say I'm not human at all?"

"No, you are not. Like me, you are of the purest blood. You do not possess any human DNA at all. I did not convert you to wolf, *l'amore*. I just awoke the wolf already hidden within you. The spell you were under that repressed your memories and abilities would have worn off soon anyway. I just needed to claim you before it did. I couldn't take the chance that my enemies would find you first."

"You have enemies?"

"Why else would you suppose I order you not to leave my sight or this floor? It is not a matter of trust. I trust you implicitly. You cannot be an alfa and lived for as long as I have and not have acquired a few enemies, Amanda."

"I didn't really think you were serious about that. I thought you were just trying to force me to your will."

He shook his head, but a slight smile remained. "I

would prefer your cooperation, *sì*. You are also an alfa, and it is in your nature to fight if I try to force my will upon you. Not that that wouldn't be fun or a challenge, but your safety is first and foremost in my mind. This Friday is the full moon, and until after the ceremonies, you are vulnerable. You have not yet transitioned and have not come to full powers yet. My enemies could take advantage of your weakness in an attempt to destroy me. I am strong and do not worry much about myself, but you...you, I do not wish to lose."

Marco winked at her again and picked up the phone, punching in the numbers as Amanda watched. "Rafael—*Sì, ho bisogno dei vostri servizi—Sì—Sì—Essere qui in due ore.*"

He handed her the phone. "Invite your friend to lunch. Rafael will be here in two hours."

Amanda took the phone. "Marco, are you sure about this?"

"*Sì.*"

"What should I say to her?"

"Tell her I've invited her to go to Ember's with us."

"Embers...that's a little pricy for lunch."

"I thought women liked pricy restaurants."

"We enjoy good food and good company. Although going to a fast-food restaurant isn't my idea of a good time, you don't have to try to impress us with the cost of the meal, Marco."

"The cost of the meal is irrelevant. Embers has excellent steaks. So unless you have objections to the cuisine, then call Caroline."

"No, steak is fine." She took the phone. "Caroline.... I know you just left my office.... Nothing's wrong...Marco has invited you to go to lunch with us." Amanda held the phone away from her ear as Caroline squealed. "I guess that means you'll go?... Good. Be ready in two hours. And Caroline? Fix your makeup before we go.... Why? Uh, don't ask why. Just do it. Trust me.... Okay, we'll meet in the lobby at one."

"It's all arranged." Amanda stood to leave.

"Where are you going?"

She shrugged. "Back to my office, I guess, to try to get some work done before we leave." Marco smiled, shaking his head no. "I'm not going back to my office?" He continued to shake his head. She sat back down. "Okay, is there another project that I'm supposed to be working on?"

His eyes darkened as he loosened his tie. "We have two hours."

Amanda glanced at the door and slid to the edge of her seat, ready to take flight. "Marco, no...not here."

He hung his suit jacket on a hanger, then turned to her, slowly unbuttoning his shirt. "Yes, here." Amanda shifted in her seat. The mental images he was sending her bent over his desk as she rode his cock had her fidgeting with sexual tension. "I told you yesterday what I was going to do to you next time you were in my office."

"Yes, and the mental pictures you're sending me now are a pretty vivid reminder." She licked her lips, watching his muscles contract beneath the open shirt as he unfastened and unzipped his suit pants. "You also said you'd rip the clothes from my body...." She swallowed hard as she watched him lock the door, then advance toward her. "I don't have any more clothes here."

"Yesterday, I took the liberty of stocking the closet for

both of us, and this office has a private bath with a shower." Amanda stood in front of him, and their eyes met. "Do not run from me. My wolf will want to give chase."

"I don't back down from a direct challenge, either."

Marco slipped his arms around her and cupped her ass in the palms of his hands, bringing her hips flush with his. He rocked his hips into her soft flesh as she pressed her body to his, and draped her arms around his neck, then their lips met in a brief kiss. "I've been waiting all day to have you," he said as he nipped her neck. Marco lifted her, and she moaned, wrapping her legs around his waist as he carried her to the desk and placed her on the edge. He knelt down and ripped the buttons from her blouse, then peeled the pants from her hips.

Marco looked up into her eyes, his dark with need. "I can smell your arousal, *tesoro*. My wolf wants his mate."

Amanda nodded. "Mine too."

Marco ran his fingers over her mound of soft curls. They were wet to his touch. She ground her hips into his hand as he slipped two fingers deep between the folds of her nether lips, and she moaned as he stroked her deep. "I need to taste you. Drape your legs over my shoulders and lay back on the desk." As she lay back, he continued, "I want to watch you roll your nipples between your fingers while I feast upon you." He watched her as she cupped both breasts in her hands, taking her nipples between her fingers, pinching and pulling at the tender buds. He pushed her legs further apart and added a third finger into her sheath, and suckled as his lips devoured the pebbled nub between her legs. She moaned, rocking her hips again, soaking his fingers and chin. He added his tongue and continued to pump as she continued to writhe on the desktop for him. Removing his fingers, he plunged his tongue deeper as she rocked into his mouth, uninhibited. Gathering her cream on his finger, he ran it along the seam of her ass and breached the tight opening as she clenched her teeth together to keep from screaming out his name as she came hard.

He stood and stroked his cock. "My God, Amanda, I have never seen a more beautiful sight than the one before me."

Amanda sat up and smiled, then pushed him back into his chair. "My turn, *la mia Alfa Lupo*." Dropping to her knees, she wrapped her fingers around his thick cock and stroked. He caught his breath as she ran her tongue from base to tip, then took the head into her mouth as she continued to stroke with her fingers.

"*Mio Dio*," he groaned, surging his hips forward as she took more of him into her mouth. Bobbing her head, she took him deeper and deeper as he continued to surge forward. Amanda had never taken pleasure in doing this before. She found herself wanting to please Marco the way he had pleasured her. Knowing he was close, she cupped his balls with her other hand and rolled them with her fingers as he surged a final time, nearly choking her as he came. He was still fairly hard when she withdrew her mouth from his cock and traveled up his body to cover his mouth with a kiss. She straddled his hips, her knees on either side as she pressed her body to his, his tongue seeking and exploring her mouth. She pulled back just enough to suckle his bottom lip into her mouth.

"*Mio Dio*, woman. You are insatiable, and I feel like I'll

never get enough of you, either…I want to bury my cock deep inside that tight pussy of yours and fuck you until neither of us can walk." Amanda smiled and swayed her hips. Marco growled, "You wish to tease your mate?" Amanda rocked her hips again, teasing his cock.

Taking her by the hips, he stood, bringing her with him. She giggled as he turned her around to face the door. "Bend over the desk, l'amore…this isn't going to be as slow or gentle as I wanted it to be." Marco pushed her shoulders down toward the desk, forcing her to lean on her elbows. He spread her legs, exposing her bare backside.

She looked back at him over her shoulders and wiggled her hips tauntingly, and felt her juices run down her leg.

Marco growled, then plunged his cock all the way in. He froze when she sucked in her breath, and was tighter than he expected. "Have I hurt you?"

Amanda shook her head, expelling a long breath. "No." She laughed softly, looking over her shoulder at him again playfully. "I was so busy teasing you that you took me by surprise." She wriggled her hips again, and he brought the palm of his hand down on her backside. "Hey!"

A growl of "Behave" had her giggling and wriggling her hips one more time.

Amanda heard the word "Mine" running through his mind, and her wolf answered in a growl, "Mine."

Marco nipped at her shoulder, then ran his fingers over her clit. Amanda sucked in her breath as a wave of pleasure pulsated through her body.

"Yes, l'amore, we belong to each other—always," he said as he steadied her hips, then withdrew his cock to enter her again. This time he didn't stop when she moaned his name. His cock stretched her, filling her completely as she surged her hips back to meet each powerful thrust.

The connection was stronger between them this time, and she could feel what he felt: the slick tightness, the heat, the tingling building from deep within. The pleasurable combination was driving her close to the edge as she felt his desire build with hers. When Marco grazed his fingers across her clit again and then sank his canines into her shoulder, she felt her body quake around him, drawing him in deeper, milking him, as she felt both their bodies explode in mind-boggling sensations.

Amanda felt his weight over her. His head cradled against her over her shoulder. She turned her head and kissed his cheek, sighing out the word "Mine."

Marco stood, then sealed the wound on her shoulder with his tongue. Turning her to face him, he took her into his arms, rocking her gently.

She snuggled deeper. "Why was I able to feel what you felt, too, this time?"

"It was because your wolf came to her mate willingly this time. Our souls are now as one. If you concentrate, you can *feel* what I am feeling at any given moment." He hugged her tighter. "*Ti amo, Amanda, così tanto.*"

Feeling warmth surround her, she looked up at him. "You love me?"

Marco kissed her forehead. "*Sì.*"

Amanda swallowed hard. "I feel a deep connection to you...but love?" She shook her head. "I don't know if the feeling is love or simply lust."

Marco smiled, grazing a finger across her cheek. "I have waited three hundred years for you. I can wait a little longer to hear the words." He laughed softly when she tried to withdraw from his arms, then he winked, lessening the mood. "Although lust is a good start."

She shoved him away and then smacked his shoulder, a grin forming on her lips. "I walked into that one, didn't I?"

Marco tilted his head, broadening his smile. "*Sì*, you did." He winked again. "I heard every word you said to Caroline earlier, and you *were* holding out before."

"Was I?" She stepped back into his arms and wrapped her arms around his neck, brushing a light kiss across his cheek. "This could prove to be interesting."

He threw his head back, letting out a bark of laughter. "You, woman, I will never tire of." He hugged her tighter, then kissed her forehead. "We better get cleaned up, or we're going to be late for our lunch dates. It could be a little inconvenient if they come looking for us."

~*~

Marco ushered Amanda through the doorway in the back of his office into an enormous, elegant bathroom. She stepped into the center of the room and looked around. It contained a dressing area, a walk-in closet, a large stone tiled shower with showerheads in the ceiling, and two walls. Running her fingers over the stone exterior, she smiled, then glanced at Marco. "Wow. I thought my office was nice." She turned toward Marco, spreading her arms out wide. "But this is beyond my expectations." Amanda glanced at the shower again, then back to Marco. "Do the Glasko's offices have rooms like this as well?"

Marco chucked her under the chin, brushing his lips briefly over hers. "I'm glad you like it. I designed it with you specifically in mind. I haven't had the need to use it until now." He ran his hand across the stone wall as he inspected the workmanship. "No, the Glaskos do not have a private bath and dressing room. Although they did look at me strangely, they didn't question my decision to add the room since, technically, it was my money, and I am their boss."

Amanda furrowed her brow. "Yeah, I'm still having difficulty wrapping my mind around that one.... How long exactly have you been a silent partner in this business?"

"For about three months."

She bit her lip and studied him. "That's about the time when I found my apartment."

He nodded. "*Sì.* I'd been searching for you for months. Then one evening, you happened to show up in my nightclub with that boy toy on your arm."

"Jeffrey."

"*Sì.*" Marco took two towels off the shelf, handing her one. "I thought you to be a beautiful woman, nothing more, until I caught your scent. I had to refrain my wolf from ripping the other man's throat out. I knew then that you were the mate I had been searching for...the one from the legends. Shortly thereafter, I made sure you became aware of the apartment for rent."

"That explains how I just happened onto a deal I couldn't refuse on an apartment." He nodded. "Hmmm, that reminds me of another topic that's been kind of bugging me since we met."

"What is that?"

"I was under the assumption that our kind were very protective of their mates."

"*Sì*, we are, *l'amore*."

Amanda clutched the towel to her breasts. "I don't understand...you didn't do anything to Jeffrey."

Marco smiled. "I didn't?" When Amanda shook her head, he laughed softly. "I could not fault the man for desiring a beautiful woman." Amanda's mouth dropped open. "But, I could not allow him to remain in your life, either. The woman you call Clair was easy enough to compel. I did nothing to Jeffrey but compel her to flaunt herself to him. It was his choice to take what was offered. And he had been taking advantage of her charms for a couple of months before you walked in and caught them in the act." Amanda narrowed her eyes, gritting her teeth together. "Had he not been a 'smart' man, I would have had to resort to more drastic permanent measures."

"You mean kill him?" Marco nodded. "Had I known he'd been sleeping with Clair as long as he had been, I would have probably killed him myself." She jerked her head away from his hand when he reached to brush a hair from her cheek. "I should be pissed at you...." His expression fell as he let his hand drop. "But I'm not. I still do not understand why you waited—"

"I had not marked you yet," he interjected, "and could not do so until the time was right. It was not an easy task for me to allow your relationship with the human to continue until you were ready to be mine."

"Oh, so if I desired to take Jeffrey back, then you'd allow it?"

Amanda laughed when Marco's eyes glowed, and his

canines dropped. "No, mine," he growled.

She patted his cheek, then reached in to turn the water on. "Just checking."

"It works both ways, *tesoro*."

She placed her towel on the bench, glancing back at him as she turned to step in under the water. "What works both ways?"

"Being protective. You will want to kill if another woman touches me."

She smiled as she stepped under the water, then yanked him in behind her, barely giving him time to toss his towel. "I already am protective," she said as she stepped into his arms, taking his cock in the palm of her hand and stroking.

Marco growled again and buried his nose in the crook of her neck as he thrust his cock in her hand. He licked the vein there and followed it all the way up to her earlobe, suckling it into his mouth. "Keep that up, and we will be late."

Amanda reached over, grabbing the soap from the dish and lathered him down. The soap had her hand sliding easily as she washed and teased him at the same time. "It's a pity we don't have time to finish this—"

As soon as the words left her mouth, in a single fluid movement, Marco had her braced against the wall and had his cock buried deep within her. "We will make the time," he said as she wrapped her legs around his waist, and all thoughts of time fled her mind. He helped support her weight as he took her hard.

The slick friction of the soap and water had her holding onto his shoulders tightly, writhing and tightening her pussy around his cock. Each plunge filled her completely, touching the spot that drove her to abandon any thoughts other than the feel of him between her thighs. She felt her canines drop and an uncontrollable desire to taste him. She gave in and sank her teeth into his shoulder, taking him into her as her world exploded around her.

Marco roared out his own release as her climax had her pulsating around him.

Amanda's legs were shaking so bad in the aftermath that she released them slowly from around his waist, and he allowed them to travel down his body to stand on the shower floor. He kept his hands around her waist to support her.

She ran her fingers lightly over the ragged wound as the blood ran down his shoulder. She looked up into his eyes as hers brimmed with unshed tears. "I'm sorry—"

He kissed her forehead. "Don't be sorry. I'll wear it proudly."

"But it has to hurt. You're bleeding…bad. And it looks like it'll leave a nasty scar."

He barely gave his shoulder a glance before he smiled at her. "It will leave a scar," he said as a tear slipped out of the corner of her eye. Marco wiped it away with his thumb. He then tilted her chin and brushed her lips with a soft kiss. "You have marked me as your mate."

"What?"

"I bear your mark as you bear mine. It is the way of our kind. All will be able to sense that we've claimed each other as mates."

Amanda couldn't understand how he could be no nonchalant about it all. From what she could see, she had punctured an artery or something. The blood now ran down his arm, turning pink as it pooled in the water. She panicked. *Dear God, I've killed the man*, screamed through both their minds.

Marco threw back his head and laughed.

Amanda shoved him away from her and ran to the bath towels on the bench. She grabbed one, shoved Marco against the wall, and applied pressure.

"Amanda, what are you doing?" His voice was still filled with humor. "Now, the towel is wet."

"I don't think this is funny. I'm trying to save your life, and you're worried about me getting a fucking towel wet."

Marco reached up and peeled the towel and her hands away from his shoulder. "We heal quickly, as you already know."

"I thought so too, but the bleeding hasn't slowed down any. You'll die—"

"I won't die, *l'amore,* at least not from a bite from my own mate. Although we are not immortal, our lives can be ended by another wolf, but our life spans are eternal. That means we won't die unless another causes our death. I told you before that, as my mate, you cannot harm me. The reason I am still bleeding is because the bite of a wolf isn't an ordinary wound, and our bodies don't readily heal on their own from the bite. We have healing agents in our saliva. Run your tongue over the wound, and I will heal before your eyes."

Amanda didn't hesitate…she ran her tongue over the tattered skin and watched the blood stop and the skin knit back together before her eyes. A scar did remain, but not nearly as severe as she thought it would be. "Thank God," she said as she pulled him into a fierce hug and let the towel drop to the floor.

He laughed softly as she stepped back to look at his shoulder again. "You didn't believe me?"

"You're laughing at me."

"It's just that I find your innocence in our ways to be refreshing. Don't ever change, *tosoro*. You are perfect the way you are."

"Perfect," she said as she stepped back under the stream of hot water. She poured some shampoo into the palm of her hand and lathered up her hair. "I am far from perfect, Marco." She leaned back and rinsed the soap from her hair.

Marco's fingers followed the line of bubbles trailing down her body.

Her nipples pebbled, then her eyes flew open. "No, take a step back, mister. We are running late enough as it is, and I, for one, do not want to explain why to Caroline."

"Rafael will already know." Amanda flushed as she stopped and stared at him as he continued. "We are *lupo*. He will be able to tell from our scents. No amount of soap or perfume will disguise what we have done or our desire for one another."

She shoved the shampoo into his hand and stepped out of the shower. "I could have gone all day without that tidbit of information." She grabbed the towel, running it briskly over her body. "Great, now I'll never be able to look the man in the eyes."

CHAPTER TEN

"*Invio, la porta è aperta, Rafael,*" Marco said as he slipped his arms into his suit jacket. He winked at Amanda as the door opened, and Rafael stepped inside.

Amanda picked up her purse, placing the strap over her shoulder as she studied the man who had just entered. He was dark complected like Marco and nearly as tall. Unlike Marco, his features were rugged but charming, and his muscular build was a little bulky for the suit he wore. He looked like the type that was more comfortable in a "wife-beater" and a pair of jeans. She smiled. *Caroline is going to trip over her own tongue*, she thought.

"*Marco, io sono qui,*" Rafael said as he closed the door behind him.

Marco nodded as he gestured toward Amanda. "English, please, Rafael. A young woman will be joining us, and I do not believe she speaks our language."

"No, she does not," Amanda said and stuck out her hand. "Hello, Rafael. I am Amanda."

Rafael smiled, nodding toward Amanda. "She is a wolf," he said as he took her small hand in his and brought it to his lips, eliciting a growl from Marco.

Amanda withdrew her hand, placing it behind her back, then rolled her eyes at Marco as he stepped between them.

Amanda huffed, "This is unbelievable."

Rafael's grin grew as Marco pulled Amanda to his side, then tucked her behind his back. "I did not intend to harm her."

When Marco growled again, Amanda stepped around him and smacked him on the arm. "I'm sick of this macho crap today. Behave!"

Rafael took a step back as he caught her scent, the smile dropping from his face, his eyes widening in surprise. "She's an alfa."

"*She* is your queen," Marco said sharply.

Rafael dropped his head in obedience to his alfa. "I am sorry, sire. I thought that she was the woman you called me in to meet. You had not informed me that you had found your mate."

Marco crossed his arms over his chest. "You should have known by her scent the moment you crossed through that door...she bears my mark."

Amanda shook her head. *Marco, stop it. It was an honest mistake.* She stepped toward Rafael to place a comforting hand on his shoulder, but Marco's growl had her pause and retract her hand. She glanced up at Marco before she spoke; his eyes were glowing red as he glared at Rafael. "Rafael, you didn't do anything wrong to apologize for." Marco's glare turned to her. She glared back, raising an eyebrow in challenge as she continued to speak to Rafael. "You are his enforcer—"

"He is right, my queen. I should have known by your scent as soon as I walked through the door. I have been remiss in my duties, and I am fortunate he did not rip my throat out for touching his mate…enforcer or not." Rafael dropped to one knee. "Forgive me."

Amanda crossed her arms over her chest, glaring back at Marco. *Forgive him, Marco.*

It is not my forgiveness he is seeking. It is yours.

She frowned. *I don't understand…he has done nothing to me that needs forgiveness.*

It is a direct insult to touch a mated female without requesting permission to do so.

But I stuck my hand out to him….

I had not granted the permission.

Amanda blew out a puff of air in frustration. *What? You mean to tell me that if you don't give permission, it is a direct insult to me?*

Marco nodded. *Yes.*

I'm still so confused. There is no logic in that explanation.

The red faded from Marco's eyes when he smiled. *It is our way, tesoro.*

That is a very stupid rule.

It prevents misunderstandings.

Like this one?

Yes.

If I forgive him, will you?

Yes, but later, Rafael and I will have a very serious talk about his dereliction in his duties.

He wouldn't have been derelict in his duties had you explained 'wolf protocol' to me before he arrived. You're faulting the man because he didn't catch a scent the instant he walked through the door? Marco inclined his head. *Marco, that's just stupid. He is supposed to be among friends.*

In his position, he is supposed to be diligent at all times. One mistake at the wrong moment could get us all killed.

Come on, Marco, Is it really that bad out there? Isn't this taking it all to a bit of the extreme?

Yes, it is that bad out there, and no, I don't think it is. I told you before that I am concerned for your safety.

I've not noticed anything suspicious. Are you sure?

Our kind all know the prophecy, l'amore.

Okay, so?

They all know that when I mate, I will rise to power and rule over all, and all will answer to me. There are a few packs that wish to ignore the prophecy and will go to any lengths to prevent this from happening—including killing you.

Not that I don't trust you. I just find that a little hard to believe. I've lived a pretty normal life.

They've already tried once. Amanda's eyes widened as he continued. *A group of elders took you from your parents to hide you when they heard the rumors to destroy the babe. Your parents were killed by the other pack when they refused to disclose your location.*

Mom told me on her deathbed that I'd been adopted and my biological parents were dead. I didn't know for sure if I believed her or not. She was terminally ill with brain cancer...I thought it could have been the illness talking. It wasn't, was it? Marco shook his head, no. She took a quivering breath. *You're telling me that they're still out there and still hunting me, aren't you?*

No, that pack has since been hunted down and destroyed,

but they weren't alone, and we have no firm knowledge as to who exactly the others are. So in the meantime....

Amanda raised her chin a notch. *In the meantime, I lay low and stay by your side.*

Yes, and don't be overly friendly with anyone you don't know.

Marco, Rafael....

Rafael will be granted a little leeway because you wish it... but I'm still going to address this with him.

She nodded. *Thank you. You still have to go over all this with me. Tonight would be a good time. I don't want to get anyone else in trouble.* Marco nodded.

Amanda blew out a breath. "Although I am still very confused about all this, Rafael, I forgive you."

"Thank you, my queen."

Amanda glanced up at Marco when Rafael still hadn't moved.

Tell him to rise.

What?

It is our way.

Oh, for Pete's sake. Amanda threw out her arms. "You may rise."

~*~

Amanda's cell phone vibrated. She pulled it out of her pants pocket and laughed as she read the text out loud to Marco. "Caroline wants to know if we left without her."

Marco smiled. "Tell her we'll be right out to meet us downstairs by the elevators."

She sent the text to Caroline. "Good, I'm starving," she said as she hit the send button.

Marco let out a bark of laughter. *Worked up an appetite?*

Amanda felt the flush travel clear down to her toes as she shoved the phone back in her pocket and headed toward the door. "Men," she said under her breath.

As Amanda stepped out into the lobby, she heard the men speaking low behind her as she headed toward the elevator.

"The young woman you are about to meet is a human."

"I should have guessed as much. You wish me to be discreet...."

"Not particularly. She is a close and loyal friend of my mate. The human knows about our kind. I am pretty sure she will assume that you are a wolf, as well."

"I see. You wish me to court her to please our queen then, I assume."

Frowning, Amanda whirled around to face the men. "You assume wrong."

Marco held up his hand to Amanda. "No, Rafael, this is not a forced arrangement. All we wish is for you two to meet. Nothing else."

Rafael studied the couple. "So if I don't like her...."

"Or if she doesn't like you," Amanda countered.

He shrugged. "I can walk away?"

"Yes," she said as she pushed the elevator button. The doors opened, and they stepped inside.

Rafael sighed heavily. "What's wrong with her?"

Amanda and Marco glanced at each other and then back at Rafael. "What's wrong with who?" Marco asked.

"The woman. There has to be something wrong with her for you to play at matchmaking."

"The woman has a name," Amanda said sharply. "Her name is Caroline, and there isn't a damn thing wrong with her. She's beautiful and funny…and…loyal to a fault." She jabbed her index finger at his chest. "And she knows nothing about this. We did not tell her that Marco invited you along as well, so be nice."

"She is definitely an alfa," Rafael said in a low voice to Marco.

"'She' has ears and can *hear* you," Amanda growled.

Marco laughed as Rafael took a step back from Amanda.

Rafael cleared his throat uncomfortably. "I did not mean that the way it sounded. Being an alfa is something to be proud of. My apologies, my queen, if it sounded otherwise."

Marco shook his head. "You might better quit while you're ahead, Rafael."

"Agreed," he said to Marco, then turned to Amanda. "I will be a perfect gentleman."

"No, all I ask is that you be yourself," she said as the doors opened. "Caroline's not really into the suit and tie kind of guy anyway."

Amanda stepped off the elevator and stopped dead in her tracks. Caroline was standing across the room with Charlie, and they appeared to be in a heated argument. The security guard had left his post and was headed their way. A small crowd had also gathered. "Uh oh, trouble," she said under her breath.

She heard Marco sigh heavily, then glanced up at him. He loosened his tie a little. "I better go break it up."

Amanda stayed Marco by placing a hand on his arm. Her eyes widened when she caught a few of the words. "Wait.

They're arguing about us." He nodded, then continued in that direction.

Rafael pointed in the direction of the commotion. "Is that the woman I was brought here to meet?"

"Yes. Sorry. It's not one of her better moments."

The corners of his mouth turned up in a smile as he continued to stare. "*Lei è magnifica.*"

Amanda glanced over at Rafael, noticed the smile, and smirked. "Tell me something." Rafael inclined his head but continued to watch. "Is it a wolf thing?"

Rafael did look at her this time. "Wolf thing?"

She shrugged. "It seems like every time a woman gets pissy around you guys, it turns you on." Rafael threw back his head and laughed. "I don't find this situation funny or attractive in the least, yet you men seem to thrive on it. Why?" Amanda pointed back toward the commotion. "What do you see that I don't?"

"You're referring to Caroline?"

"Yes."

"I see passion."

Amanda stared harder. "All I see is anger."

"*Sì,* there is that too, but to be able to express herself in such a way shows the passion she is capable of from within. She will love and make love as fiercely as she argues. To possess a woman with such high spirits assures us that life will never be boring in or out of bed."

"Ah, so it's a sex thing."

Rafael laughed again. "Not entirely, but *sì.*"

"I figured as much," Amanda said absently as she watched the scene seem to escalate. "I better go over there and see if I can help."

"I better join you. Marco looks as though he's ready to kill the human."

"You arrogant asshole," Charlie yelled as he surged forward toward Marco. "You can't fire me."

Marco raised two fingers, and two security officers grabbed Charlie's arms. "*Sì*, I believe I just did."

Charlie fought against the restraints. "I will sue you. I will own this pathetic company when I'm finished with you." As Amanda reached Marco's side, Charlie's face twisted in a sneer. "And you, *bitch*, will pay as well."

Marco growled.

Amanda elbowed him. *Don't.*

He has threatened you.

He's just being his charming self. "Charlie, as usual, you are letting your mouth overrun your brain."

"I will sue you both for sexual favoritism."

Marco growled again. "You do not know what you're talking about."

"Don't I?" Charlie sneered again. "Amanda, I dare you to deny that you're fucking the boss. Come on, deny it."

Amanda caught her breath as she felt every eye in the crowd land on her.

Marco slipped his arm around her, pulling her close to his body. "Of course, she's sleeping with me." He kissed her on top of her head.

Amanda's breath wooshed out as her mouth dropped open in horror. *Tell me you didn't just say that.* She looked up at Marco, and he winked.

"I knew it!" Charlie jerked on his restraints again as he

looked around the crowd wildly. "You all saw that. She has that guilty look like her dirty little secret has been exposed, and you all heard him admit it too."

"She is my wife."

Amanda caught her breath again. *What?*

Charlie seemed to deflate. "What?"

"I said she is my *wife*," Marco said a little louder.

"I don't believe you."

"You can believe whatever you wish, but disbelief doesn't make it not so."

Charlie shook his head. "No, it has to be a lie. The staff would have been informed."

"And we had planned to do so at Monday morning's staff meeting. We were going to announce that we are now married, and Amanda, as my partner, is a majority owner in this advertising agency."

"As I said, favoritism."

"I bought my share of this agency for her. She is the best asset that this agency has ever had. The Glaskos agreed and sold me the majority shares. Our marriage was destined long before I did so. So favoritism? No. I figured it was a good investment."

Charlie sneered again. "There is no way I'm accepting that she's my boss now."

"And you don't have to." Marco nodded to the security guards. "You've been fired, remember?"

Charlie jerked on his restraints again. "On what grounds?"

"Insubordination...disturbing the peace...inciting a riot...false accusations. Any one of these is grounds for immediate dismissal. Take him up to his office," Marco said to the guards. "Help him pack and escort him to his vehicle."

"Yes, sir."

"You can't do this," Charlie screamed as they forced him toward the elevator. "Let go of me." The doors opened, and he was pushed inside. "You haven't heard the last from me," he yelled as the doors closed.

"Show's over," Marco said to the crowd.

Rafael watched everyone disburse. "That one is going to be further trouble."

Marco nodded. "I'm sure he will be."

Caroline tapped Amanda on the shoulder to get her attention. "Married?" she asked as soon as their eyes met. Amanda bit her lip when Caroline raised an eyebrow. "Since when?"

"It's just a small technicality," Marco replied to her question.

She nodded. "In other words, you made it all up."

Marco smiled. "No, not entirely. You are not completely ignorant of our situation."

She nodded. "I am aware of a little."

"We will finish filling you in over lunch."

"Good. I was afraid lunch had been canceled."

"No, I believe we all need to leave this building and let things settle." Marco gestured toward the door, ushering everyone in that direction. "Mr. Granger has caused quite a commotion."

"Charlie's an ass," Amanda grumbled.

Caroline laughed. "I agree." She nudged Amanda and whispered, "Who's the hunk?"

"Your lunch date," Amanda whispered back.

Caroline stopped in her tracks, causing Rafael to bump into her from behind. "What?" She looked up as Rafael smiled back at her. She flushed when he winked.

"Mandy...."

Amanda laughed at her expression. "It's just lunch, girlfriend, and you begged...."

Caroline's eyes saucered. "Hush," she interjected before Amanda could finish. "A little warning would have been nice...I just made an ass of myself back there."

Amanda laughed harder. "Caroline, this is Rafael."

Rafael smiled and brought her fingers up to his lips. "It is nice to meet you, Caroline."

She flashed a smile at Amanda. "He's Italian."

"He is."

Caroline turned to Rafael and broadened her smile. "It's nice to meet you too."

"Rafael, she's a bit of a flirt," Amanda said.

"Mandy!"

"Well you are."

Rafael laughed, placing his hand on the small of Caroline's back and nudging her toward the door. "I am somewhat of a flirt myself at times. Lunch with this beautiful woman should be interesting."

Caroline giggled. "Ooh, I like him already."

Marco winked at Amanda as she laughed at her friend. He had them stopping at the security desk. "Joe, could you please call to have the company limo brought around?"

"Yes, sir, right away."

Amanda paused. "A limo?" Marco nodded. "What's

wrong with your car? I'd say we could take mine, but you made me leave it at the apartment."

"There is nothing wrong with my car, *tesoro*. It is just a bit cramped in the back seat for one the size of Rafael."

Caroline looked at them all. "*Tesoro*?"

"Sweetheart," Rafael supplied.

"Oh, that's so sweet."

Amanda shook her head at her friend. "Caroline—"

"Well, it is, girlfriend." She grinned and nudged Amanda. "What endearment do you call him?"

Amanda flushed when they all stared at her. "How did this conversation get turned around on me?" The men smiled, and Amanda shrugged. "I don't know. The only thing I can remember calling him other than by his name is 'asshole.'" Rafael threw back his head and laughed as Marco shook his head. Amanda shrugged again and said, "Sorry. That was totally uncalled for."

"Yes, it was," Caroline supplied. "You can do much better than that. Just think about the way he makes you feel."

Marco smirked, staring at her expectantly.

Amanda smiled back at him and bit her lower lip. "Makes me feel...hummm...the term *Amante* comes to mind."

When Marco's smile broadened, Caroline looked at the group in question. "*Amante*?"

"Lover," Rafael supplied. "A fitting name for a mate."

"Mr. De Lucia, your limo is out front," Joe said.

"Thank you, Joe," Marco replied. He placed his hand on the small of Amanda's back as they approached the limo. *I like the sound of Amante as it rolls off your tongue.*

She looked up at him and smiled as she slid into the

limo. *I have to admit that it does sound a bit better than asshole.*

Marco laughed as he slid in beside her. *It does.*

Rafael helped Caroline onto the seat across from Amanda and Marco. She shook her head and said, "I get the feeling that they have entire conversations that I can't even hear."

Once Rafael was seated, the driver closed the door. "They do." Caroline's mouth gaped. "True mates can speak with each other through their minds."

"No shit," she said in disbelief. "Mandy, you can do that?"

"Yes."

"Why didn't you tell me?"

"I haven't told you a lot of things. So much has happened to me in the last few days. I'm still trying to sift it all through my mind."

"Wow, that's a pretty amazing trick."

Rafael took Caroline's hand in his and squeezed her fingers. "I may teach you how someday."

"Rafael," Marco said in a low voice and shook his head no.

Amanda looked up at Marco. *What?*

He is moving too fast.

He's just holding her hand.

It is not what he did. It's what he said.

I still don't see that he's said anything wrong.

He is implying that they may become mates.

Amanda's eyes widened. *Can they even do that? She's human.* When Marco smiled, she rolled her eyes. *I don't mean have sex. I'm not a total moron. I know they're capable of that. You know you have me wanting to call you "asshole" again.* Marco's grin broadened. *I mean, are they capable of becoming lifemates?*

It is not done often, but some mate outside our species. Yes, it is possible...a human can be converted.

Converted? Marco nodded. *Converted how?*

You've heard the legends.

You mean the stuff they put into books and movies? He nodded again. *He would have to bite her?*

Yes, but not just a small nip. He'd have to tear into her flesh.

Like I did to you in the shower?

Something like that, but to a human, it can be very painful... some humans do not survive the conversion.

Amanda glanced at the couple and saw Caroline staring at her expectantly. *He can't be serious...to want to hurt her.*

He doesn't want to hurt her. He must have really been impressed with her to even imply such a thing.

Why?

We mate for life. It is not something we take lightly.

Caroline is somewhat of a free spirit and flirts a lot. She will need to understand everything and be given a choice.

I'll make sure of it.

How are you going to do that?

I am his alfa. He has to obtain my permission before he can take a human for a mate.

No one asked my permission.

You were already a wolf, tesoro, and you had already been given to me by prophecy and by your parents.

My parents?

Sì, the contracts were signed when you were conceived.

Contracts...they still do that kind of medieval stuff?
Our kind does, sì.

Caroline had been watching Marco and Amanda interact since the moment Marco had said Rafael's name sharply. Rafael had continued to hold her hand but had become silent. She squeezed his fingers to get his attention. "They're talking about us, aren't they?"

Rafael glanced at his alfa before he answered her. "I would assume so, *sì.*"

"You mean, you don't know?"

He hesitated before he replied. "It's complicated, *piccolo.*"

She smiled. "*Piccolo.* What does that mean?"

"It translates to 'little one.'"

Her smile broadened. "*Piccolo,* I like that."

Rafael smiled in return. "Have you lived in Chicago long?"

She shrugged. "All my life. Have you? I've never seen you around."

He glanced at his alfa again. "Only for about the last hundred years or so." Caroline gave him a blank stare. "I've mostly been by Marco's side since I've been here. It hasn't left much time for socializing."

"Did you just say a hundred years?"

"*Sì,* I was sent here from Italy to be Marco's enforcer. I had been trained to do so from the time I was a small pup." Caroline started shaking her head, no. "It took me nearly fifty years to master the English language."

Caroline disengaged her hand from his and brought both her hands up to form "time out." "Woah, give me a second here."

Amanda leaned forward and placed her hand on Caroline's knee. "Take a deep breath, sweetie."

Her eyes saucered as she stared frantically back at her friend. "But he's a wolf."

Amanda nodded. "He is...and so am I."

"Yeah, but—"

"He has feelings just like you do."

Caroline shook her head, feeling helpless.

Amanda squeezed her knee. "He is more loyal than any of the other guys you've dated." Caroline nodded as Amanda continued. "And I would have never agreed for you two to meet had I thought you wouldn't be safe with him."

"I would never harm you, *piccolo*," Rafael said.

Amanda patted her knee again, then sat back in her seat. "I understand what you're feeling, girlfriend. I was there myself just yesterday." She looked up at Marco and smiled. "These men have a way of changing a woman's mind." She turned back to Caroline. "If you're still afraid after we finish our lunch date, Rafael has agreed to leave you alone." Caroline nodded. "All I ask is that you agree to keep an open mind."

"Okay."

The limo pulled to a stop at the curb, and the driver got out and opened the door. Amanda smiled up at Marco as he put out his hand to help her out. "Thank you," she said as she stepped to his side. She watched Rafael exit, and the only word she could think of to describe his expression was deflated.

Rafael helped Caroline exit the limo, but she didn't meet anyone's eyes...instead, she stared at the ground.

Marco spoke to the hostess, and they were taken into a private dining area. Amanda held back. *Marco, I'm going to take Caroline to the ladies' room.*

I've never understood why a woman feels the need to take another woman into the bathroom with her.

Caroline's not acting like herself, and we need to have a talk—alone.

I don't want you two running off alone. Remember our talk earlier.

I think it's worth the risk. I don't want those two miserable this entire lunch. I'll make it as quick as I can. Tell Rafael not to give up.

If you say so. We'll order for you. You have five minutes.

Oh, for Pete's sake, Marco. Five minutes?

I'm sorry, tesoro, but we're not in a secured building.

She sighed. *Whatever,* then nudged Caroline. "Come with me for a minute."

Caroline looked up. "Where are we going?"

"To the ladies' room. We need to talk—alone."

"I don't know what good it's going to do, but okay."

Caroline followed Amanda into the ladies' room. Amanda made sure they were alone, then locked the door. She whirled around on Caroline. "What the fuck is wrong with you?"

Caroline backed up. "Huh?"

"You did a complete 180 in the limo."

Caroline shook her head. "No...I didn't...I—"

"You what?"

Caroline sat down on a high-back chair and hung her head. "I don't know what's wrong with me. I guess I'm disappointed."

Amanda threw out her hands. "In what?"

"Rafael."

"I didn't see or hear him do anything to you, girlfriend. You seemed to actually *like* him, so there has to be something—"

Caroline jumped up and scrubbed her fingers through her hair in frustration and started pacing. "I *did* like him, okay? Geez!"

"Then what did he do to disappoint you?"

Caroline threw out her hands. "He didn't *do* anything. It's me. It's all me. I guess I got my hopes up too high because I actually thought I might of found a guy I could relate to."

Amanda sat down on one of the chairs and draped one leg over the other. "Spare me the bullshit, baby girl. You're pissed because you just found out that he's not human. Admit it."

"Okay. I admit it! Geez!"

"Caroline Robinson! I never thought I'd see the day that you would be so cruel."

"What? Is it so wrong of me to want to stop the fantasy before it gets out of control?" She started pacing again. "I'll admit that he's a nice package to look at...and he knows the right things to say."

"And he made your heart flutter."

She stopped in her tracks and shook her head. "He didn't."

"He *did*. I heard it." Caroline continued to shake her head. "If you were truly not attracted to him, *we* wouldn't be in the bathroom discussing this right now. This morning your words gave me a lot to think about, and now I believe it's time for you to follow some of your own advice. Go with your first instinct and give the guy a chance."

Caroline shrugged. "What's the point? We have no future. He's not human."

Amanda pointed to the empty chair. "Sit down. I need to tell you something."

Caroline plopped down in the chair. "What?"

"Rafael's reaction when he heard he was to meet you was pretty much the same as yours when he found out you were human."

"You see?"

Amanda shook her head. "No, baby girl, I don't. He was prepared to dislike you from the getgo, but I watched his expression the first time he saw you. You were fighting with Charlie—"

Caroline snorted. "I bet that was attractive, with me yelling at that bonehead."

"Rafael thought so. As he stared at you, he was smiling. He said, '*Lei è magnifica.*'"

"What does that mean?"

"It translates to 'she is magnificent.'"

"He said that?"

Amanda nodded. "He did. I even asked him what he saw in you."

"What did he say?"

"He said he saw a beautiful woman with passion and spirit. And with a woman like that, life would never be boring." Caroline stared at the tiles on the floor. "He even hinted to taking you as his mate."

Caroline's head snapped up. "What?"

Amanda stood. "He thought enough of you to consider the possibility of having you as a lifemate...then you hurt his pride when you shunned him for something that he cannot help."

"That something puts a pretty wide gap between us."

"Why? Why is it necessary to put up barriers?"

"Amanda, he's not *human*. Even if I wanted to, there is no future for us. I'd just wind up getting hurt—again."

"I'm going to give you a little food for thought. Wolves mate for life." Caroline looked up. "Marco said that a few take humans for mates."

"They do?"

"Yes. So if that's all you're objecting to, I want you to get out there and have a good time. If it works between you, then that's great. If it doesn't, don't let his being a wolf be the reason to walk away. The reason needs to be that you just aren't attracted to him, which I know for a fact is a lie." Caroline stood, and Amanda gave her a hug. "A little word of advice from my own personal experience. Wolves are better at sex than human men are."

Caroline pulled back and smiled. "Nu uh."

Amanda held up her hand and smirked. "I don't lie about good sex." Caroline laughed for the first time since entering the restaurant. "What? You said you wanted to live your sex life vicariously through me." Amanda laughed with her. "Just kidding. No, you need to live it for yourself." Caroline nodded. "Are you feeling better?"

"Yes."

"Good. We better get back to the table before Marco busts down the door looking for me. My five minutes are about up." Caroline gave Amanda a strange look as Amanda pushed her through the doorway. "That's an explanation for another time."

"Amanda, that sounds seriously fucked up."

"It's not what you think."

"Oh, and you know what I'm thinking now?"

"No, but I can guess because I'd be thinking the same thing if I didn't know the reasons behind it."

"But—"

They rounded the corner to the private room. "I'll tell you later, but just so you don't stew over it during lunch, it has something to do with the prophecy and my safety."

Both men stood as they walked into the room. Amanda caught Marco's gaze and winked. *We're good.*

Marco smiled and held out the chair for her. "We've ordered lunch."

Amanda sat down, and he pushed the chair in. "Thank you."

Amanda watched Rafael. His expression hadn't changed from earlier as he held the chair for Caroline as she sat. He pushed her chair in and sat back down, placing his hand on the table.

Caroline smiled. Reaching across the table, she placed her hand over his, squeezing his fingers until he looked up. "Thank you, handsome."

Rafael turned his hand over, lacing her fingers with his. The corners of his mouth slowly turned up in a smile. "Why don't we start over?" Caroline's smile grew. "Hello, Caroline. I'm Rafael...."

CHAPTER ELEVEN

Marco sat back in his chair and took a sip from his glass of wine. He watched Amanda place her fork back down on her now-empty plate. *That is quite a change in Caroline.*

Amanda smiled. *It is.*

Tell me, did you have to compel her? Because I don't believe Rafael would want it that way.

No, I...what?...wait.... Her eyes widened. *I can do that?*

I am not sure. It is a power that you will have once you ascend. Whether you have it now or not is questionable.

Amanda glanced at the couple, quietly talking. She was happy for them both. *No, I didn't stare into her eyes and command her to do anything.*

What did you say to her?

What, you weren't listening?

He laughed softly. *No, I was busy talking to Rafael.*

She smirked. *In a nutshell, she was just worried about getting hurt. She figured that since he wasn't human that she had better stop the fantasy now before she got hurt.*

And?

Amanda shrugged. *I told her that a relationship was*

possible and to not let his being a wolf be the deciding factor on whether they should date or not.

Good. I'm sure he will ask me later if you used compulsion.

You can honestly tell him that I did not.

Marco looked up. "The waiter is coming. Do you want more wine?"

"Do you think I should? I still have work to do, and today has been a wash. I might as well have been off. I've not accomplished anything workwise, and there's a big presentation next week—"

Marco placed his finger over her lips, halting further protest. "Yes, more wine, please."

Caroline laughed and held up her glass to be filled as well. "I probably shouldn't either, but hey, I'm with the boss, right?" Everyone laughed in agreement as the waiter filled her glass.

The waiter stepped back and hesitated, a look of indecision marring his features. "Mr. De Lucia...there are three individuals out front who demand to speak with you."

Marco and Rafael exchanged a quick glance. Marco slid his chair back. "Did they say who they were?"

"The woman said her name was Katja Wolf and that she was expected. She declined to give her companions' names."

Marco and Rafael exchanged glances again. "Send her back."

The waiter nodded, then left the room.

Amanda sat back in her chair. "Who is Katja Wolf?"

"I'm sure we're all about to find out."

"You mean, you don't know?"

"No."

"But the waiter said she was expected."

"I was not expecting anyone. I do, however, know the name 'Wolf.' I fought a battle with a pack over in Germany about three decades ago. I saved their alfa from an ambush. His name was Heiko Wolf."

Rafael nodded. "I also remember that battle. Heiko would have lost his head had you not intercepted the blade."

Amanda sat forward on the edge of her seat. "What kind of ambush?"

"An ambush is a group of tigers. Heiko had managed to piss their leader off by killing one of their guards. It was just a misunderstanding, but the ambush didn't see it that way and sought revenge."

"And who is Katja?"

"I have no idea who she is, but I am almost certain she is part of Heiko's pack. Maybe he needs my assistance again."

Rafael sat back in his chair and regarded Marco. "It does seem odd that they would send a woman."

"Agreed. It is odd."

Amanda's mouth dropped open when a beautiful blonde woman stepped through the door. The woman's eyes lit on Marco. She smiled and spread her arms wide. "*Marco, meine lange verloren Kumpel. Ich bin hier.*"

Rafael's eyes saucered as Marco choked on his wine.

As Amanda pounded on Marco's back, she looked to Rafael for an explanation. "Rafael, what did she say?"

"She called him her long lost mate."

Amanda's response was instant. The two guards flanked Katja's side when Amanda whipped her head around and brought her upper lip back in a snarl, exposing her extended canines. "*Mine bitch,*" was drawn out in a low growl.

Katja laughed. "You, *Hündin*, are just a minor irritation."

Caroline caught her breath as Rafael yanked her chair closer to him. "Rafael, what's happening?"

"Our queen is challenging this newcomer for her mate." Rafael smiled in admiration. "*Lei è l'essenza di nobiltà.* The woman does not seem concerned. She threw the insult back at her."

Caroline smacked him on the arm. "Well, don't just sit there. Help her."

"I cannot."

"But Amanda doesn't know what she's doing. She doesn't know how to fight."

"It's instinctive, *piccolo*. She is an alfa, and she has marked Marco as her mate. If the woman doesn't back down, Amanda will go for the kill purely on instinct." Caroline bounced in her seat and opened her mouth to object. "If Katja's guards try to interfere, I will step in."

Marco wrapped his arms around Amanda, pulling her to him. *Remain calm, tesoro.*

She cannot have you. You are mine.

Sì, I am now and will always be.

Who is this woman?

Calm down, and we will find out.

If she lays one finger on you, I will bite it off.

Marco regarded the three at the end of the table. "You seem to have us at a disadvantage. The only mate I have is the one in my arms."

Katja stepped forward, thrusting her chin arrogantly in the air. "*I* am your rightful mate."

Amanda growled again, and Marco held her tighter. "Amanda is the only mate I have ever had—or want."

"*I* belong to you, not *her*." When Amanda yanked at her restraints, the woman laughed. "You need to control your *Hündin*, Marco, before I have to put her out of her misery."

Caroline elbowed Rafael. "What's a *Hündin*?" she whispered.

"It is German for 'bitch.'"

"Ooh!" Caroline said indignantly. "That's the pot calling the kettle black."

"Shhh, *piccolo*, you are not a wolf. Keep your voice down unless you think to challenge her yourself." Caroline shook her head.

"I don't care who you *think* you are to me, Katja," Marco said, "but you and your friends need to leave us. You have worn out your welcome."

Other than a smile spreading across her features, Katja didn't move. "Think hard, *mein Kumpel*. I have nothing but time."

"I have no knowledge of what you're referring to, Katja. There is nothing to remember."

"You know my father, Heiko."

"Ah, I figured that you must be related."

"Yet you still shun me. That is not very hospitable of you, *mein Kumpel*."

"I am not your mate, Katja. Stop calling me that."

"Ah, there, you are *wrong*. You were promised to me on my birth."

"If that is true, someone promised you something that was never theirs to give."

Katja's chin jutted higher in the air. "Are you calling my father a liar?" Her companions tensed up, extending their claws at her tone.

Rafael stood, bringing Caroline's chair with him as he stood beside Marco's chair.

"I have not seen nor heard from your father in three decades, Katja. He used to be a fierce and mighty alfa, fair and just. We parted as friends. That is all I can say to speak for his character."

"So, you deny saving his life from the ambush?"

"I do not deny it."

"You know our laws as well as I, *mein Kumpel*. When you save another's life, they are indebted to you. He was *obligated* to give you something precious to him. It happened to be *me*."

"Go home, Katja. Tell Heiko that I release him of his obligation."

"That is a direct insult to my father," Katja yelled. "I would go home in disgrace. I won't do it."

"Again, I tell you to *go home*, Katja. Even had I not found my mate, I would not have accepted you." She spat on the floor and glared at Marco. "I had already been promised to Amanda by prophecy. However, I would have chosen her even without the prophecy."

"Do you think I care about prophecy?" she screeched.

"You should. It governs our kind."

She slammed her hands on her hips and stamped her foot. "I only care about claiming what is rightfully mine."

"You have traveled a great many miles for nothing, Katja. Go home. Your father is free to mate you to another."

"I do not want another. I choose you!"

When Amanda growled again, Marco stood and tucked her behind his back. "Leave!" He pointed toward the exit. "You have worn out your welcome. If my pack catches any of you in my territory again, you will be destroyed."

"You threaten me?"

"It is a promise."

Rafael stepped forward, baring his claws and fangs.

Katja took a step back this time. "Fine, we will leave, but you have not heard the last of this, *mein Kumpel*. You will regret sending me away."

Marco pointed forcefully toward the door again. "Now, go!"

CHAPTER TWELVE

"You have not heard the last of this, *mein Kumpel*. You will regret sending me away," Amanda mocked as she straddled Marco's hips and sat down, draping her arms around his neck. "Who does that bitch think she is?"

Marco laughed softly at Amanda's antics as he placed his hands on her hips. "Had I not already been mated by our laws, I could have been obligated to be with her."

"Over my dead body."

Marco sobered. "That *was* her intent today."

Amanda shrugged. "Again, those are very stupid laws," she said as she kissed the tip of his nose.

He chucked her under the chin with his forefinger. "They are the laws we have lived by since the beginning of time. Again, they prevent—"

"Misunderstandings," Amanda supplied, then tossed her long hair over her shoulder. "Yeah, yeah, we've been over that one before. It doesn't mean I have to agree with it, *Amante*." She leaned forward, running her tongue along the vein in his neck to his earlobe, then rolled her hips tauntingly over his swelling cock.

"No, you do not, but you do have to live by them, *l'amore*." When she rolled her hips again and nipped at his neck, he laughed softly. "You are not paying attention to a word I'm saying."

She flashed him a smile. "If what you're saying doesn't have anything to do with having sex with me, then my ears are closed," she said, swaying her hips again to stress her point.

Marco growled low, then flipped her over onto the oversized couch in his apartment. The shirt she wore, his shirt, fell open, exposing her bare breasts. He smiled. "Ah, a feast fit for a king."

She brought her hands up to her breasts and rolled her nipples between her thumbs and forefingers, puckering the rosy peaks for him. "Make me squirm for you, *Amante*," she said.

He bent down, drawing the puckered peak between his lips, suckling hard, drawing the flesh deep into his mouth. She held his head to her while he suckled first one, then the other, and moaned as a seated need coiled between her legs.

Marco moved up her body as he lowered his lips over hers. The kiss began as gentle but progressed to hungry as she opened her mouth, and he plunged his tongue inside, stoking both their hunger. She moaned again and bucked her hips as his hand slipped between her thighs, sliding three fingers deep into her dewey depths, causing Amanda to writhe beneath him. Her own fingers joined his, both plunging faster as her world tumbled out of control. His lips withdrew from hers, and his whispered "cum for me" had her screaming out his name in release as her pussy pulsated around his fingers, soaking him with her juices.

He withdrew his fingers and brought them to his lips. "Your taste is the sweetest nectar," he said as he sat up on his knees, spreading her legs wider. Raising her hips with the palms of his hands, he said, "Cum for me again," then plunged his tongue deep inside her. Amanda screamed as her body bowed up off the couch and quaked in his hands. Her fingers grasped the couch cushions in a frantic attempt to stabilize her world as waves of sensations rolled over her.

"I love how your eyes glaze over in the heat of passion. I will never tire of seeing you this way."

Amanda opened her eyes, and a lazy smile formed on her lips as her gaze traveled over his body. She admired his muscular chest, tapering down to ripped abs. Thick and ready, his cock stood out, straining from his body, a pearl of cum seeping from the tip. "I shall never tire of seeing you this way, either."

He watched her eyes travel down his body to stare at his cock, and it twitched and strained toward her. "Do you like what you see, *innamorata*?" There was so much more he wanted to do with her body, but his wolf wanted release.

"Yes, *Amante*." She wrapped her fingers around the swollen member and rubbed the purple head over her clit.

Marco clenched his teeth at the sensations as the swelling in his cock grew. His wolf growled low. "My wolf wants to fuck his mate," came out in a low growl. "He cannot wait until you transcend so he can have her."

"My wolf wants her mate as well," Amanda said as she continued to rub his cock over her wet swollen nub. "Oh, who am I trying to kid? It's not just my wolf. It's me. Fuck me,

Amante. Teach me how to howl for you."

"You will howl," he growled as he pushed her knees forward, and she guided his cock into her opening. Their eyes locked. "You will howl out your release as I cum inside you," he said as he rolled his hips in a hard thrust, plunging his cock deep within her pussy. Amanda moaned as she felt each glorious inch stretch and fill her, barely touching her sweet spot, to withdraw and surge forward, again and again, a little deeper with each stroke. She felt Marco's soul merge with hers as it had done earlier that day. Again, she felt what he felt, a hot, slick wetness surrounding the sensitive head and shaft in a tight grip, where the slightest movement felt like heaven. She wrapped her legs around his hips, locking her feet, drawing him in as she rocked her hips with his, their bodies moving as one, his cock sliding in and out faster as the tense tingling built within them both. She felt her control slip, howling long and loud as he buried his cock to the hilt and stilled while her body attempted to suck him in deeper, her own release taking her to teeter on the peak, milking his cock as her inner walls spasmed around him. Marco howled out her name as they both plunged over the edge.

Amanda awoke a few minutes later with Marco's weight still covering her body. They both had a light sheen of sweat cooling their bare skin. She nuzzled his neck, kissing the soft juncture at the base. Closing her eyes, she rubbed her cheek against his stubbled one, sighing a contented, *"Ti amo,* Marco."

He propped up on his elbow and smiled down at her. *"Ti amo più."*

She laughed softly. "You cannot love me more than I

love you because my heart bursts with it."

"You told me this morning that you felt lust, not love."

Her smile grew. "Somewhere in between this morning and now, I have changed my mind. Maybe it was the moment I realized I could lose it all when another tried to steal you from me."

"You are stuck with me, *innamorata*. We mate for life, and to our kind, life can be a very, very long time."

"I will hold you to that," she said playfully, then pushed on his chest. "Get off me, big boy. I'm hungry."

Marco nipped at her neck. "Woman, you are insatiable, and that would require me to remain where I am."

She shoved again. "For food, *Amante*," she said, laughing harder. "I have worked up an appetite, and I need the energy to keep up with you."

He stood, then held out his hand to help her up. Amanda grabbed his shirt on the way up and placed a quick kiss on his lips. Turning on her heel, she headed toward the kitchen and hid her body from Marco's view by sliding the unbuttoned shirt over her shoulders and letting it drape over her curves.

"To hide that luscious body from your mate is cruel, *innamorata*," Marco said as he sat back down on the couch. A smile formed on his lips as he watched her butt cheeks play peek-a-boo from beneath the shirttail as she walked. Then Amanda grabbed the shirt collar and slid the shirt halfway down her back, looking over her shoulder as she playfully danced toward the refrigerator. "You're such a tease. Come back over here, and we will pick up where we left off."

Amanda laughed. "I hope your refrigerator is better

stocked than mine is," she said, opening the refrigerator door, "or we'll be ordering delivery."

"I haven't been staying here much, so there is probably not much in there."

Amanda peered inside, then turned to face him. "Not much there?" He shrugged. "It's empty. I thought you said you came over here this morning to get the eggs."

"I did. That was the only food I had in the apartment. I will send Rafael to the grocery store tomorrow to stock the refrigerator."

She placed her hands on her hips. "Well, in the meantime, you have a very hungry mate on your hands."

Marco stretched out on the couch, then patted the cushion beside him. "I can think of plenty of things to do to occupy your mind."

Amanda snapped her fingers. "I'll be right back."

Marco sat up straight. "You're leaving dressed like that?"

Amanda shrugged. "Don't get up," she said as she placed a bottle of wine on the marble countertop. "I'm just slipping through to my apartment. I still have the cheese ball and beef stick from the basket you gave me unopened in my refrigerator. And I believe I have some crackers in the cabinet. The only thing you had in your refrigerator was this bottle of wine, so if we pool our resources, it'll tide us over until *we* can go grocery shopping."

Sitting back on the couch, Marco scrubbed his fingers through his hair. "Grocery shopping?" He made a face and shook his head no. "I—"

She flashed him another smile. "Since you won't let me

go anywhere without you right now, you will go to the store with me."

"No, I said we will send Rafael."

"No, *we* will not send Rafael. I do my own shopping, thank you. You will either go with me, or I will go by myself, but the bottom line is I'm going with or—"

"Fine," Marco cut her off. "I will go. I do not know what I am griping about anyway. Once you transcend this weekend, a bodyguard will no longer be necessary."

"Thank God," she said as she opened the pantry door, pushing the button. The wall slid back, opening into her darkened pantry. She glanced over her shoulder and winked. "I'll be back in a couple of minutes." Marco nodded.

Amanda pushed the pantry door open and stepped into her kitchen. The overhead light was on. "That's strange," she mumbled. "I could have sworn I had shut the light off." She glanced around the kitchen and didn't see anything out of place. "Hmmm, guess not."

She turned back toward the pantry, and reaching up on a shelf next to the refrigerator, she plucked a box of crackers off the shelf, then placed them on the counter. As she reached for the handle on the refrigerator door, the lights went out. Whirling around, she plastered her back to the kitchen counter. *Someone's in here with me*, raced through her mind. Reaching behind her, she groped for one of the knives in the wooden block as the tiny hairs on the back of her neck prickled. Her fingers wrapped around one of the handles as she withdrew the knife from the block. *Why didn't the backup generator kick in, Marco?*

What are you talking about?

You still have lights?

Yes...you do not?

No. Amanda took a quivering breath. *I don't think I'm alone.*

Do not move, tesoro. Amanda heard a slight noise to her right. *I see you by the counter. Please do not stab me.* She heard the amusement in his voice. *Although it would not kill me, it would hurt like hell.*

"I don't think this is funny, Marco," came out in a harsh whisper.

Shhh. Do not speak aloud. You were correct. I can smell other wolves in your apartment. He sniffed the air. *I do not recognize their scents.* He tensed, then growled.

Marco?

"Except for one," came out in a loud growl. "Show yourself, Katja."

Amanda shielded her eyes when the lights suddenly came on. The kitchen was surrounded by men carrying guns and wearing gas masks. Katja stood in the center with her mask pushed up on top of her head. Amanda's eyes widened as Marco started to shift.

"I wouldn't do that, *Liebhaber*." Katja purred. "The bullets in these guns are made of the purest silver. You, of all people, know what silver will do to our bodies."

"I will never allow you to take my mate, Katja."

"*Allow*." Katja threw back her head and laughed. "I am in charge here."

Amanda grabbed Marco's arm to stay him. The guns were raised and pointed in their direction. *Marco, don't.*

"This is an act of treason, Katja," Marco growled low,

his claws sinking into the wood cabinetry. "In a few days, I will be king."

"King," Katja continued to laugh. "Yes, as *mein Kumpel,* you will rule over our pack beside me as alfa. My father never quite recovered from a separate attack from the ambush and is a feeble shell of the mighty wolf he once was. As the alfa, I rule now."

"You will doom your pack to certain death, Katja. This will start a war."

A few of the men lowered their guns and backed away.

"*Enough,*" Katja yelled. "Stand your post."

"*Aber Alfa....*" one of the men stuttered.

"Dissension in the ranks, Katja?" Marco taunted.

"Shut up, *mein Kumpel,*" she growled, then raised her arm to lower her mask. "Now, Hector."

A silver canister bounced onto the kitchen floor. Yellow smoke swirled into the kitchen with a strong sulfur smell. Amanda reached for Marco as her world suddenly went black.

Chapter Thirteen

Drip...drip...drip....

Amanda reached up, clamping her palms over both ears in an effort to drown out the incessant noise. The pounding in her head, amplified a thousand times, pierced through her skull with the sound of each drop. She was cold, and her entire body ached from her position on the hard floor. A moan escaped her lips as nausea rolled over her. If the pounding didn't stop, she was going to throw up.

Marco.

Nothing.

Marco.

Still nothing.

Her mind was in a fog. The effort it took to remember how she got on the floor had her head pounding harder. *Why isn't he answering me*? raced through her mind. "Marco," she said aloud and clamped her palms tighter against her ears, the sound of her own voice bouncing painfully off her eardrums.

A seated fear clutched her heart when he still didn't respond. "*Marco*," she yelled. "Oh, God," she moaned as she rolled into a fetal position, then her body spasmed in dry heaves.

Everything went black.

~*~

Amanda peeled an eye open, then reached up and shielded her eye from the glare of the overhead fixture. Her eyes hurt, but she was beginning to get her bearings—at least the nausea was gone. She pushed herself up onto an elbow, then scooted to a sitting position to lean her back against the cabinets. Her limbs felt lethargic, but for the life of her, she couldn't remember why.

She opened the other eye, then slowly lifted her head to look around. The kitchen looked like a tornado had touched down. Cabinet doors hung askew. Some were splintered, and others were broken and scored deep with claw marks. The refrigerator door hung broken, teetering from the bottom hinge, the interior light flashing on and off erratically, reminding Amanda of a horror movie she'd seen. Her heart ached. This wasn't a movie. Tears slipped out of the corners of her eyes as she stared at the broken glass mixed with blood that littered the floor around her. It was obvious that a huge fight had taken place, but Marco was nowhere to be seen.

"Marco," she attempted again.

Silence.

Looking down at herself, she realized that she, too, was covered in blood, but it wasn't hers. She searched for some memory as to how any of this could have happened— her mind was drawing a blank. Amanda pulled herself to her feet, staggering to the kitchen island, dragging her feet to avoid stepping on glass. Leaning heavily on the broken countertop, she scanned the living room. It appeared much like her kitchen. Most of the furniture was knocked over, and some torn to shreds. The glass to the sliding doors leading to her balcony was shattered, leaving the curtains flapping in the breeze, giving glimpses of a low glow of light forming on the horizon. *"Marco! Where are you?"* she yelled. Silence answered her.

Amanda glanced over her shoulder toward the open pantry. A glow of light beckoned from the other side. She scanned the floor and took a huge step over the glass to reach her destination.

Sliding through the opening, she stepped into Marco's kitchen. The cold bottle of wine she had placed on the counter was still there. However, the bottle was at room temperature when she reached out and touched the glass. "I remember the wine," she said as she scanned the empty room. "Think, Amanda...think...think about what happened." The memory of the evening they shared earlier came flooding back to her. A ghost of a smile touched her lips as the scene on the couch replayed in her memory. Then she remembered being hungry and coming into the kitchen—she scowled when the memory stopped on that damn bottle of wine.

"Marco, where are you?" she demanded as she turned a full circle in the room. She reached up to run her hands through her hair in frustration and ran into a snag. Swallowing hard, she thought of the scene in her kitchen. Running the matted hair between her fingers, she pulled the clump of hair into view—blood. She took a quivering breath. "This better not be his," she mumbled, dropping the matted clump. "No, I'm pretty sure I'd feel it," she placed her hand on her chest, "if he were hurt or dying," she said under her breath, then yelled at the room at large, "Wouldn't I?" Again, no response.

Amanda slipped the ruined shirt from her shoulders and dropped it into the trash can on her way to the bathroom. A shower was a necessity because she couldn't leave the apartment in her condition. She was bound and determined to get to the bottom of this—today. If, on the off chance, he needed her help, she would be there for him. Marco could be pissed or not, she reasoned, but she was leaving without him.

Amanda stepped into the steaming spray. Red rivulets of watered-down blood trailed from her body, pooling at her feet, then running down the drain. She lathered and scrubbed three times before she was satisfied that all traces of the blood were gone. A short time later, she was dressed in her clothes from the day before, and her hair combed, laying damp against her neck. There was no way she was walking back through her apartment alone to get clean clothes. These would have to do.

Grabbing her purse, she fished out her cell phone, then threw the strap over her shoulder. The time on the phone read 5:30. She debated for about a half a second, then pulled up Caroline's number and pushed the send button—no answer. Amanda really needed to talk to Rafael but had no idea how to reach him. Shoving the phone in her pocket, she stepped out into the hallway, closing Marco's apartment door behind her. Not wanting to be seen, she took the main elevator to the second floor and then took the service stairs to the parking garage.

She walked past Marco's car in the garage on her way to her own. Chills ran down her spine with the knowledge that he didn't leave on his own. The quest to find Rafael took on a new urgency. As she slid into her car seat, she dialed Caroline again...still no answer. *"Shit!"* Throwing the phone on the seat next to her purse, she inserted the key, firing up the engine. Amanda backed out of her spot, then squealed the rear tires as she punched the gas.

Caroline's apartment was only ten minutes from hers in traffic. This early in the morning, she made it in five. Parking her car on the street by a parking meter, she didn't bother with change because she had no intention of staying long. As she stepped out of her car, she scanned the area for anything suspicious before she slammed the door and jogged up to the front entrance.

Caroline's building didn't have the same security that hers did, allowing her to walk right in and straight to the elevators. "A lot of good the security did me last night," she mumbled, the twisted irony striking her as she stepped inside the elevator and rode up to the third floor.

Boom, boom, boom. The door shook as she pounded her fist against it. At this moment, Amanda didn't care if she woke the entire building. She heard the muffled sounds of Caroline's feet rushing across the room and a quiet "Who's there?" from the other side.

"It's Amanda."

The door flew open. Caroline was on the other side with her hair tousled, wearing an oversized man's shirt buttoned up wrong, and she didn't look the least bit tired. "Amanda!"

"It's Marco," Amanda said breathlessly.

"What about Marco?" Amanda heard Rafael say as he stepped out of Caroline's room, wearing only a pair of jeans.

Amanda only hesitated a second as she looked between

them, then brushed past Caroline into the apartment to stop in front of Rafael. "He's gone."

Rafael put up his hands. "Take a breath and tell me what happened."

Amanda scrubbed her fingers through her hair and started to pace. "I don't *know* what happened."

"What do you mean you 'don't know?'"

Amanda threw out her hands. "It's like my memory has been erased somehow."

"Start from what you can remember...this is important."

Amanda nodded nervously. "Okay," she let out a shaky breath. "I woke up this morning on my kitchen floor with a splitting headache. I was covered in blood, and my place was a wreck...and by wreck, I mean destroyed." Caroline placed her hands over her mouth as Amanda continued. "I tried calling out to Marco through our link, and he didn't answer. I cannot remember what happened. My last memory was of the night before, and Marco was there. Now he's...not."

"Can I touch you?"

Amanda stopped in her tracks. "What?"

Rafael kneeled before her. "I need your permission to touch you."

Amanda shrugged. "If you think it'll help."

Rafael stood, placing the palms of his hands on her temples and closed his eyes. He frowned, pressing harder. "Someone has placed a block on your memories."

"Who would do something like that?" Caroline asked.

"Someone who doesn't want her to find Marco." He withdrew his hands, then let out a long breath. "I need to see your apartment."

"I figured you would, and I tried to call first, but I really wasn't sure how to get ahold of you."

"You could have called me," Caroline said.

Amanda nodded. "I did...twice—no answer."

Caroline shook her head. "No way," she said as she walked to the table and picked up her phone. "Oh, my God! Two missed calls?" She held out her phone. "How did that happen?"

Amanda took the phone and flipped it over. "The ringer is turned off."

Caroline took her phone back and hugged Amanda. "I'm sorry. I didn't know."

"It's okay, sweetie."

Rafael stuck out his hand. "Amanda, please hand me your phone." She placed it in his hand. He opened it and started typing. "I'm putting my number in your contacts, and I will add yours to mine. We need to be in constant contact until Marco is found." He handed Amanda back her phone and pulled his own cell phone out of his pocket, flipping through his list of contacts, then pressed the button. "I'm calling in reinforcements." He nodded to Caroline. "Baby, you need to go get dressed. We have to go." He walked away and started talking on the phone.

Amanda smiled at Caroline. "Baby?"

Caroline shrugged, a smile spreading across her face as she watched Rafael walk away. "Yeah, great, huh?"

"Yes. I'm happy for you both."

Caroline hugged Amanda again. "Thank you," she whispered, then slipped from the room.

Rafael turned his phone off and stuck it in his pocket.

"Two elders and about six other pack members will be at your apartment in about half an hour. We're going to see if we can sort this out and find out what happened to our alfa."

"Good. Thank you...I'm worried about Marco."

"I am worried as well, my queen," Rafael said as he pulled a t-shirt over his head. "However, I am convinced that he is alive. You are soul mates, and if something life-threatening had happened, you would feel it...even with a memory block."

"I had thought about that too, and that's the only reason I haven't panicked yet," she said. "I just don't understand why I can't contact him now."

Rafael sat down as he slipped on his boots. "That concerned me too," he said and looked up. "That is why the elders were called in. They might be able to provide us with reasons or solutions to our problem."

~*~

Amanda pulled her car back into her parking space. She slid out of the car and shut the door as Caroline and Rafael exited from the other side. Amanda shrugged. "What now?"

Rafael pointed to the end of the parking garage, where two SUVs were approaching. "They are here," he said as he motioned for the SUVs to continue in and park. "We will wait for them to park and go up together."

Seven men and one woman exited the vehicles and approached Amanda as a group. "My queen," Rafael said, "I'd like you to meet everyone. These two over here are two of our elders. The woman is Clara, and the man beside her is Adolfo." Both nodded to Amanda.

Amanda inclined her head. "Nice to meet you both."

Rafael motioned to the six men standing as a group, all of them tall and well-muscled. Amanda wondered briefly if being an Italian Adonis was a prerequisite to being a wolf. "Before you are some of Marco's best warriors. I'd like you to meet Alonso, Catjetan, Edmondo, Fausto, Raul, and Rico." They knelt before her when their names were called.

"It's nice to meet you," Amanda said nervously. "You all may rise."

Clara broke out in a smile. "Very good, Alessandra. I see that Marco has begun your instructions."

Amanda flushed. "Yes, ma'am, but very little."

"You were born to it, so it will not take you long to adapt." She approached Amanda and gave her a tight hug. "I was your mother's mother. You are my granddaughter, and you have grown to be a lovely woman like I knew you would."

Amanda pulled back and studied the woman in front of her. Amanda had her cheekbones and the same slant to her eyes. Amanda raised a brow. "Alessandra?"

Clara nodded. "It was the name given to you at your birth. We all thought it best to change it to Amanda when we were forced to put you into hiding."

"Marco didn't tell me I still had family living, and part of the pack no less. Hmmm...grandmother, huh?" Clara nodded. "What do you want me to call you?"

"I would prefer Nonna, but if calling me that makes you feel uncomfortable, you can simply call me Clara."

"Nonna, it is."

Amanda stepped back and took a deep breath, then addressed everyone. "I'm sure you all know that Marco is missing. Rafael has informed me that someone has tampered with my memories. I'm hoping that with all your help, we'll find Marco." She motioned for everyone to follow.

Clara put her arm around Amanda. "We will find your mate for you, *piccolo*."

Amanda nodded. "I hope so," she said to Clara.

As they reached the elevator, she turned and faced the group. "My apartment is on the penthouse floor. Marco's is next door. Mine is...a wreck," her voice broke.

Caroline grabbed her, hugging her tight. "It'll be okay, baby girl. You'll see," she whispered.

Amanda nodded, then whispered back. "I want to believe that." She let go and stepped back as the elevator doors slid open. "I'm glad you came, too."

"I'm always here for you and always will be."

Everyone filed into the elevator, and the only sounds on the way up were the mechanical workings of the machine. Amanda chewed on her bottom lip as she stared at the metal doors. Although she was anxious to find Marco, she wasn't too excited about seeing the destruction of her apartment again. The bell dinged three times as the P flashed, and the doors slid open.

The group followed Amanda to her door, where she stopped and pulled the keys out of her purse. She handed them to Rafael. "Please...I...."

He took the keys and opened the door. Amanda held back as everyone else filed in. She heard Caroline's breath catch as she crossed the threshold. Amanda made her way in, closing the door behind her.

Amanda stood next to the two elders and Caroline in

the dining room while the others fanned out in the apartment. Her eyes followed Rafael as he headed to the kitchen. When he stepped on the other side of the kitchen island, Amanda heard the glass crunch beneath his boots. Rafael disappeared behind the counter, and when he appeared again, his eyes were red.

"I know who has our alfa," came out in a low growl.

CHAPTER FOURTEEN

Amanda's hand clutched Caroline's in a tight grip as she stood frozen at Rafael's words.

Rafael's breathing grew labored, whipping his head back and forth; his breaths in and out were powerful gasps. Amanda watched in horrid fascination when claws formed and grew, cutting deep into the countertop, his entire body shaking as the fur rippled over his face and arms erratically. Rafael's face was contorted in agony as he fought the need to shift. He let out a long mournful howl that ended in a low growl.

His howl tore through Amanda's soul, kicking her into action. She let go of Caroline's hand and ran to Rafael's side.

The others gathered around as Amanda placed her hand on Rafael's shoulder, calming the beast. "Rafael, who has Marco?"

Rafael growled low. "Katja."

Upon hearing the name of her one rival, Amanda's wolf burst forth to the surface, snarling. The clothes shredded from Amanda's petite form to accommodate the girth of the huge silver wolf. She shook the shreds of cloth to the floor, adding to the debris already there. A seated rage had her seeing the room through a red haze. Teeth bared, she backed into the cabinets, snapping viciously at anyone who tried to approach.

"She is beautiful," Catjetan said in awe, then kneeled before his queen.

The other five followed suit.

"Caroline," Clara said sharply, jerking her out of her stupor. "Go get Amanda a robe from her room. Rafael, control your wolf. Alessandra is responding to you, and we need you both to focus."

Caroline ran back into the room with Amanda's robe clutched to her chest. She passed the robe to Clara.

"Thank you, child," Clara said. "Now, go calm your mate."

Caroline blinked in confusion. "Mate?"

Clara smiled as she cupped Caroline's face in her hands. "Yes, child."

"But...I'm not a wolf."

Clara's smile broadened. "You have the heart of one. Now go to him. His beast will calm to your touch."

Caroline ran to Rafael and wrapped her arms around him, speaking soothing words.

Clara approached Amanda. "Alessandra...." Amanda growled low. "It is disrespectful to growl at Nonna." Amanda hung her head. "Now that we know who is behind this, we need you to shift. There is so much work that needs to be done before we can retrieve your mate, and we need you in human form to do this." She reached out, clutched the fur on each side of Amanda's muzzle, and looked into her eyes.

"Shift, Alessandra."

Pain ripped through Amanda's body as it bowed and contorted back in shape. Her fur danced along her skin, receding in waves as the shift completed. Amanda lay huddled in a fetal position on the tile floor. Clara placed the robe over her body to cover her nudity.

Clara stood. "Alonso," she called out. "Bring two chairs in here if you can find any intact. If you can't go next door to Marco's."

"*Sì, l'anziano Clara*," he replied, leaving to go next door to Marco's apartment.

"Caroline," Clara said, "bring Amanda a glass of water."

Caroline whirled around in search of a glass, then ran from the apartment.

"Rafael," Clara raised an eyebrow, "are you recovered?"

"*Sì, l'anziano Clara.*"

She smiled and winked at him. "She is strong and held up well under pressure. She will make you a good mate."

Rafael scrubbed his fingers through his hair, shaking his head no. "*L'anziano Clara*, Marco won't—"

"Your alfa will allow it." Her smile grew. "Or he will have to answer to his own mate."

Alonso came back through the door with two chairs in tow. Caroline was close behind him, carrying the glass of water.

Alonso set the chairs down, facing each other. Clara knelt down and helped Amanda to rise, adjusting her robe as she sat up. "Come, child, sit in this chair. We have a lot of work ahead of us."

Amanda sat down and clutched the robe tightly to her body. "If that bitch harms him—"

"Alessandra, calm yourself," Clara said firmly. "Her intent is not to harm him. She only wants him for herself."

Amanda's eyes flashed red. "He's *mine.*"

Clara nodded. "He is, and we are all here to make sure it remains that way." Clara winked at Caroline as she reached for the water. She pulled a pouch out of her pocket and sprinkled the contents in the glass. "Drink this, Alessandra, and all will become clear."

Amanda eyed the glass suspiciously. "What's in it?"

Clara laughed softly. "You have such a suspicious mind, child. The glass holds the answers to all your questions."

Amanda snorted. "That's doubtful."

"Be respectful, Alessandra. You are among family and friends."

"You still have not told me what you put in the glass."

Clara let out a long sigh. "We will have to work on your trust issues."

"Pardon me, Nonna, but I recently discovered that my entire life has been a lie. So, I'm afraid it might take me a while to learn to trust again."

"I suppose I deserved that one. Very well, it's only a few herbs to clear your mind. *I* was the one who placed the original block. It was necessary for your safety to keep you hidden. The contents of this glass will remove the original block and, hopefully, the one placed on your mind last night. You'll need to drink it for us to have any hope of finding your mate."

Amanda tipped the glass to her lips and made a face.

"It tastes bitter."

"A small price to pay to get your mate back; now finish it."

Amanda narrowed her eyes. "As a child, did I even like you?"

Clara threw back her head and laughed. "You loved me."

"Somehow, I find that hard to believe."

"You are acting like a child now, so I am treating you as one. Come on. Do as you are told and finish it."

"If this doesn't work—"

"It will."

"Oh, all right," Amanda said as she stared at the glass. "This is so disgusting." She took it down in one gulp, nearly gagging. Coughing a couple of times, she shoved the glass back at her grandmother. "Now what?"

"It shouldn't be long. Your memories should begin to return, starting with the oldest ones. Tell me, do you remember your mother?"

Amanda's eyes widened. "I remember a doll in a long white dress. Her hair was black, and she had light blue eyes."

Clara nodded. "That was your favorite toy. You named her—"

"Rosa," Amanda interjected.

"Sì."

"I'm remembering Mama. She was always so happy. She played with me all the time, calling me her little Alley. One night I woke up to her yelling. She was screaming for me to run and hide. I saw Papa on the floor in a puddle of blood, and a mean man had Mama by her hair. I was too small to help, so I ran as far and as fast as I could."

"*Sì*, Alessandra, we found you the next morning."

"Yes. The bad man took Rosa for my scent."

"He did."

Tears rolled down Amanda's cheeks. "I almost wish I didn't remember."

"We could not permanently keep the memories of your mother from you. She loved you so much and would want to be remembered."

"I loved her too."

"Now, child, think back to last night. Do you remember anything?"

Amanda nodded. "I remember being hungry and teasing Marco about having to go to the grocery store."

Rafael laughed.

Amanda shook her head. "You laugh, but he wanted to send you in his stead."

"That is no surprise to me," Rafael said. "What happened next?"

"I remembered that I had a cheese ball and a beef stick in the refrigerator over here, so I came over here to get it. I was reaching for the refrigerator door when the lights went out. I remember my skin crawling and the feeling of my hair standing up on my neck. I grabbed a knife, and Marco came through the pantry and teased me about not stabbing him with the knife. He told me to not speak out loud because he could smell other wolves in my apartment. At first, he told me that he didn't recognize any of the scents, and then he growled and told Katja to show herself. When the lights came on, we were surrounded. The men were pointing guns at us, and Katja said they were filled with silver bullets. I tried to stop Marco from shifting, then they threw a canister filled with some kind of gas. That's pretty much all I remember. The apartment wasn't torn up like this when I passed out...so what happened to Marco?"

Clara took Amanda's hands in hers. "Call to him, Alessandra."

Marco.

Silence.

Amanda shrugged. "He's not answering."

"The most likely reason is because he cannot answer."

Amanda frowned. "What do you mean?"

"He might be bound in silver or locked in a silver cage. Our thought waves won't penetrate that. Silver burns us at the touch, so if he is in a cage, he will not touch the bars unless absolutely necessary."

"So, where does that leave us?"

Clara smiled. "We will perform the rites, and you will transcend."

Amanda shrugged again. "So. What good will that do?"

"The prophecies say that you will be a powerful wolf."

"So?"

"You will have the power to conquer Katja and save your mate."

"How?"

"With just a simple taste of her blood."

Amanda rolled her eyes. "Where am I going to get that?"

Rafael smiled, holding up a piece of glass stained with

blood. "Right here, my queen."

Chapter Fifteen

Amanda's fingers gripped the bottom of the chair to hold herself steady as Clara pressed harder on her temples. She felt a surge of raw power course through her veins as her body began to convulse. Pain contorted first her back, then her neck, as she felt different parts of her body shift independently of the other. One second she felt like her head was about to explode, and the next, a calming euphoria as her body relaxed.

Clara removed her hands from Amanda's temples and stepped back. "Tell me how you feel, Alessandra."

"Strange," Amanda said as she glanced around the room. "My senses are hypersensitive. I can smell all kinds of strange things I've never noticed before, and I can see dust particles landing on the table in the far corner." She tilted her head. "I can also hear Caroline's heartbeat and feel her body heat from here."

Rafael tucked Caroline protectively behind him.

The corners of Amanda's mouth turned up in a smile. "I will not harm your mate, Rafael. She is my best friend. I was just making an observation."

Clara nodded. "You are becoming one with your wolf."

"How do I keep her from bursting out like she did earlier?"

"Control is something we learn."

"Time is something I'm a little shy on at the moment."

"Once you have your mate back, your wolf will calm."

"Great." Amanda took a deep breath and then blew it out. "How are we going to use this to our advantage?"

Clara sat back down across from Amanda. "What we don't know is where they have Marco."

"How is my transcending going to help with that?"

Clara held her hand palm up. "Rafael, we need the piece of glass with Katja's blood." Rafael placed the glass in her hand. "Once you have a taste of Katja's blood, you will be able to get into her thoughts. If you concentrate hard enough, you might even be able to see what she sees."

Amanda reached for the piece of glass, plucking it out of Clara's outstretched palm. She inhaled the scent, then touched her tongue to the glass. A heady, almost dizzying sensation took over. Amanda closed her eyes. "The bitch is boasting to her pack how she has defeated me by stealing my mate and how the prophecy is wrong, that Marco is the key, and she will now rule all the packs in my stead."

"*That will never happen,*" Adolfo shouted.

Clara held up her hand. "Adolfo, calm yourself. We will make sure this does not come to pass. Alessandra, please continue."

"Katja seems to be nursing a nasty wound on her side. The blood keeps seeping through the bandages." Amanda smiled. "Marco must have bitten her and refused to heal it."

Fausto smiled as well. "At least the bitch has not broken

our alfa." Others grunted in agreement.

Clara took Amanda's hands into hers. "Now, Alessandra, we need you to concentrate. Try to see through her eyes. We need some idea as to where they are."

Amanda furrowed her brow in concentration. "I see padded chairs sitting in rows with tiny windows lining the walls. I think they're inside a plane."

"Are the other chairs filled with people?" Raul asked.

Amanda shook her head. "No, I only see other pack."

"It must be a private charter," Rafael said, "otherwise they wouldn't have been able to get Marco onto the plane. Amanda, do you see Marco?"

"No, but I do see a large square shape draped with canvas tarps in the back."

"She has caged him," Rafael said.

Clara gripped Amanda's hands tighter. "Concentrate... can you detect where they are heading?"

"I know where they are heading," Rafael said. "She is going home, back to her pack in Germany."

"How do you know this?" Adolfo asked.

"Marco and I fought alongside her father, Heiko, a few decades ago. Marco saved Heiko's life. Katja found us at Embers yesterday and confronted Marco, saying that he was promised to her by her father and that she expected him to go back home with her to be her mate. Our alfa informed her that he was already mated, but she did not seem to care. He told her to tell Heiko that he released him from his obligation, and he was free to find her another mate. To say she was upset is an understatement."

"She was furious," Amanda said, "and so was I."

"I see. Under other circumstances, Marco might have been obligated to abide by Heiko's wishes. Hmmm...." Adolfo stroked his chin in thought. "That does shed some light but does not make her actions right. Do you have any idea where this pack is?"

"It has been a few decades, but I am pretty sure I can lead us there."

"Very good. I will contact the hangar and have them ready our planes. We will send you and our queen to Germany, along with two hundred of our best wolves," Adolfo said. "If they have harmed our alfa in any way, you will destroy them."

~*~

Amanda threw an overnight bag over each shoulder as she made her way to the parking lot.

Rafael grabbed the bags from her and stuffed them into the trunk. "I thought we were traveling light," he said with some amusement.

"We are," Amanda smirked at his tone. "I only brought a single change of clothes for myself. The other bag is for Marco. He was only wearing a pair of jeans and no shoes when he came into my kitchen. If he was a wolf when they took him, he might not have any clothes at all."

"Based on the amount of blood and destruction in your apartment, he shifted."

"I was thinking the same thing."

Amanda dangled her keys in front of Rafael. "I have no clue where we are going...." She tossed the keys to him and opened the front passenger door. "So, you're driving."

Rafael slid into the driver's seat and Caroline into the

back. "The private landing strip is not far from here," Rafael said as he backed the car out of the spot and put it in gear.

"Good. We've taken too long already." Amanda looked at her watch, doing a mental calculation. "They have at least an eight-hour head start on us."

~*~

Rafael eased Amanda's car down the rocky trail flanked by dense forest. Amanda grunted when a tire hit another rut. Rafael glanced in her direction, noticing her pained expression. "We should have used my truck instead."

Amanda continued staring at the dirt road ahead of them. It seemed to stretch forever with no end in sight. "I'm not worried about the car." Frustrated, Amanda ran her fingers through her hair. "This is taking too long. Can we drive a little faster?"

Rafael steadied the steering wheel as they hit another rut. "Not unless you wish to walk the rest of the way." Amanda turned her head and raised an eyebrow. "If I drive any faster, we might break an axle. Your car was not meant to drive down roads like this."

"Fuck the car." Amanda's gaze turned to the road again. "I feel like I'm running out of time."

Rafael pointed ahead. "Do you see that bend in the road?" Amanda grunted in response. "The airstrip is on the other side."

As the car rounded the corner, the trees broke, exposing an expansive open field with an asphalt runway. At the end sat a huge hangar surrounded by vehicles. Two jets were waiting with stairs pushed up to the doors. Men seemed to dart everywhere at once in preparation as Amanda gawked.

Organized chaos ran through her brain.

Amanda gestured ahead. "How does this work, anyway?"

Rafael parked the car and turned to her. "Work?"

"Yeah, is this even legal?"

He smiled. "Our alfa keeps everything legal. This private airstrip is registered to the pack, and we file a flight plan." He winked at Caroline in the backseat. "It also doesn't hurt that some of our people work within the FAA." He opened the car door. "Caroline and I will get the bags."

Amanda threw open her car door and slid out. "Thanks," she said as she took off at a jog toward the throng of people.

Rafael and Caroline retrieved the bags from the trunk and took off in the same direction.

Clara turned and greeted Amanda. "Alessandra. Good, I am glad you have finally arrived. As soon as your bags are loaded, we will board."

Amanda gawked at her grandmother. "We?"

"Yes, the elders have decided to join you."

Amanda took a deep breath, then blew it out. "I'm sure I'm not going to like your answer, but I'll ask anyway. Why?"

Clara crossed her arms over her chest. "To be honest, it is to make sure everything remains fair."

Amanda took a step back. "What do you mean 'remains fair'?"

"From what Rafael said, this Katja Wolf believes she has a legitimate right to claim our alfa as her mate—"

"But he's my mate," Amanda interjected.

Clara nodded. "He is, but—"

Amanda shook her head. "There are no buts. She can't have him, and I will not share."

Clara rolled her eyes. "Alessandra, we would never ask you to share your mate."

"Good. You had me worried for a moment."

"But—" Clara brushed the hair back from Amanda's cheek. "We can't just kill her and her pack for no reason."

"No reason?" Amanda's mouth dropped open as she pulled away from Clara's hand. "She destroyed my apartment, erased my memory, and took my mate by force. That seems like a pretty damn good reason to me."

"She will stand trial. It is our way."

Amanda raised her chin a notch. "Adolfo said if she has harmed Marco, then they will all die."

"By trial, yes. Unless—"

"Unless what?"

"Unless she challenges you for your mate and you lose."

"By lose, you mean that I die in a fight with her."

"Yes. Then there would be no trial. We would attack without mercy."

"But I wouldn't be around to see it—great."

"No," Caroline said as she grabbed Amanda's arm.

Amanda turned to her friend. "That bitch cannot take my mate, girlfriend. You know that I'll fight to keep what is mine."

"Caroline," Clara said. "This is not your concern."

"Not my concern?" Caroline's voice went up an octave as she rounded on Clara. "Amanda is the best friend that I've ever had. I was there for her her entire life through thick and thin, as she was for me. You were not there for her while she grew up, so don't tell me she is not my concern."

"Control your human, Rafael," Clara said.

Amanda held up her hand. "Caroline's right, Nonna. She is my best friend, and the pack will treat her as such." She turned to Caroline. "I will promise you this, girlfriend. I will not do anything risky or stupid."

Clara threw out her hands. "Fine, agreed; the human has a right to voice an opinion."

"Nonna, please be nice; 'the human' is my friend, and she has a name."

Clara flushed. "Agreed," she seethed. "We will discuss this later in flight. We need to board now." She turned and stormed up the steps, disappearing into the plane.

Caroline let out a shaky breath. "Thanks, but do you really think you should have done that?" Rafael slipped his arms around her, pulling her to his side.

Amanda let out a long sigh. "Rafael, let me ask you something."

"Okay."

"Would Clara have spoken to Marco in the same manner she speaks to me?"

"No. He is our alfa."

"It is as I thought. Yes, Caroline, I believe I did the right thing by speaking up. It seems my grandmother is testing me somehow."

Rafael's eyes widened at her statement. "You could be right."

~*~

Amanda sat by a window and buckled in. It was the

first moment she'd had to herself in a while. As the plane taxied down the runway, she thought about the events of the last couple of days. She decided to try Marco again. *Marco.*

Silence.

Marco.

Again silence.

She closed her eyes and willed her mind into Katja's thoughts.

~*~

"We are here, *mein Kumpel.* Welcome to your new home."

Amanda could see Marco through Katja's eyes. He was indeed in the metal box, but now the box was in a plush bedroom. He stared out from between the bars with such ferocity that Amanda mentally backed up. Snarling, Marco charged the cage when Katja approached.

Katja threw back her head and laughed. "Ah, *mein Kumpel,* you are just upset about losing the scrawny woman. She can't possibly be any good in bed. *I* will show you what a real woman is. When I take your cock into my mouth and down my throat, I will show you how much better I am for you than that *Hündin.* You will forget all about her."

Marco snarled again. "Fuck you."

Katja's smile grew. "Yes, that is my intention."

Bitch, Amanda screamed through her mind.

Katja backed up, looking around the room. "What?"

She heard me, Amanda thought, and smiled.

"Who is listening in on my conversation?" she demanded with a stamp of her foot.

Marco's eyes widened as he got as close as he could to

the bars without touching the silver. "Amanda?"

Amanda's smile grew when he recognized it was her. *Let him go, Katja.*

"Never *Hündin!*"

Amanda felt Katja's anger and frustration, and her confidence grew. *Let him go, and I might allow you to live.*

"Allow me to live," Katja said sarcastically, then laughed. "You are just a weakling and a pest—about as worrisome as a gnat."

If I am just a small bother, then why do I feel your fear?

Katja threw her arms out and turned a circle, shouting, "I do not fear you, *Hündin!*"

You are a liar, Katja. I am in your head, and I know what lurks there.

Katja rushed over to the cage. "Get out of my head, *Hündin,* or I will make you regret it."

Amanda saw Marco sit back and regard Katja, a slow smile spreading across his face. "Give it up, Katja. If my mate is in your head, it means she has transcended. She is much more powerful than you will ever be."

"Shut up!" Katia picked up a metal rod and struck the cage. Marco didn't flinch. "That *Hündin* has no claim on you, *mein Kumpel.* You are *mine.*"

He is mine.

Katja placed her palms over her ears and shouted, "No! No, you are wrong. He is mine."

"Let me go!"

Let him go, Katja.

Katja whirled around. "Hector! Come in here and bring help! You both asked for this," Katja shouted to Amanda and Marco when Hector and three others ran into the room. "Remove him from the cage and hold him down."

What do you intend to do?

"Since you won't get out of my head, I will make you watch while I pleasure myself with his body and make him forget you ever existed."

Marco threw his body against the cage in rage, snarling as the men reached for the lock. The places where his skin touched the silver bars sizzled and smoked.

Hector was laughing, but the other three appeared nervous.

~*~

No! Amanda held her palms to her temples, her body shaking with sudden fury as her vision once again turned red. The room turned from gray to black, then overly bright.

"Amanda!" Caroline shouted.

Chaos broke out around Amanda as everything seemed to fade from her view. She blinked hard as her vision swam. When her eyes opened again, she unexpectedly found herself standing in front of Katja.

Katja's eyes rounded as she took a step back. "How—?"

"You're mine now, bitch," came out in a snarl as Amanda's wolf burst forth. Salivating and snapping her jaws, she stalked Katja into the corner, waiting for her to make a move—any move that would give her the excuse to rip her throat out.

"Release me, damn it!" Marco shouted, hitting the cage door with his shoulder again. Two screws bounced onto the carpet. Hector and his cronies backed away from the cage as Marco charged the door again. They crossed themselves and ran from the room.

"Cowards," Katja shouted.

Amanda snapped at her again for moving.

Marco struck the door again, and the last two screws gave way. The door slammed back on its hinges, bouncing against the wall.

His wolf took over in stages as Marco rose from the cage and made his way over to Amanda. She still had Katja cornered and wasn't letting her move. He stopped and stood beside his mate. Amanda's wolf was large, but Marco's wolf towered over her. When she glanced in his direction, he licked her muzzle.

She whimpered and rubbed her head against his massive chest. *I was worried about you, Amante.*

I was worried about you as well, l'amore. I am happy yet surprised to have you here.

You're not the only one—surprised, I mean. I'm still trying to figure that one out. I have a lot of questions.

His wolf snorted. *I have a few of my own. Like, where are the others?*

They are on their way here now.

How did you—?

Amanda grunted. *I was hoping you could tell me that one. One second, I was on the airplane with the others. I was messing with that one's thoughts, hoping to find out more about how you were doing and exactly where you were, then the next second, I was seeing red and standing in front of her.*

It seems we both have a lot of questions for the elders.

That one will be easy. They're on their way here now.

Why?

Amanda motioned her muzzle toward Katja. *They want to make sure that one gets treated fairly.*

Marco's eyes widened as he whipped his massive head around to look at her, his lips drawn back to expose his canines. *What?*

Funny, that was my reaction too.

I don't find this the least bit amusing.

Neither do I, Amante. Clara all but forbade me from killing that one unless she attacked me first. Amanda motioned her muzzle toward Katja again. *She calls her pack cowards, yet she cowered away from me without shifting.*

Have you had the opportunity to compare yourself to another wolf?

I'm looking at you now. You are huge.

That is because I am an alfa. I am even larger because I am now king over our kind. You would be at least twice the size of her wolf because you, too, are an alfa and my queen. To shift would be a direct challenge to you. She apparently wishes to live.

Amanda growled at Katja. *She should have thought about that before she abducted my mate.*

He licked her muzzle again. *I agree.*

Amanda glanced up at him again. *I have a question that has been nagging me since I saw you shift.*

He turned to look at her. *Ask.*

How did they manage to take you? I mean, look at you. You're huge. I would have thought they would have done what she is doing now, cowering away.

The gas affected me some as well, but I still managed to shift. I had to protect you. I even managed to take a bite out of that one. Then I felt a sting in my side, and a gun was raised to fire again. They fired three tranquilizers into me before I went down. I destroyed the man with the gun, but the drug was too much, and I passed out. I woke up in that cage over there, and the silver didn't allow me to shift. My human form was very weak because the drug lingered in my system. It was just wearing off when you appeared in the room like my avenging angel.

What matters to me the most is that you are safe and we are together again. Do you think this pack will give us any trouble?

I believe the four that ran from this room have spread the word about our threat to the pack and their alfa. If they were going to attack, a force would have been here by now. Their alfa did not believe in the prophecy and had convinced them that it was a tall tale passed from generation to generation. I believe your sudden appearance and my unexpected strength against the cage must have convinced them that the stories were true. Fear should keep them in line. So, in theory, they should comply with our demands.

Demands?

They will all stand trial before the council of elders for treason. The elders will make a ruling and decide their fate.

But you are their king. Why isn't it your decision?

Since the attack was centered on us, the other packs might consider our opinion and ruling biased. Now that I've calmed down, I can see the wisdom in the elders' commands.

Amanda shook her head. *So much bureaucracy. It makes my head spin.* She looked up at him. *What if they don't? Comply, I mean.*

He looked into her eyes. *Then we fight.*

CHAPTER SIXTEEN

Amanda shifted in stages back to her human form. She twisted her torso as she leaned over and popped her back. *Will I ever get used to this?*

Marco grunted as he sat down on his haunches. *It will always be somewhat painful, but you will grow accustomed to the pain over time.*

She reached for the cuffs hanging from the side of the cage. As soon as she touched the metal, she withdrew her hand as the contact sizzled against her skin. *"Shit!"*

Katja laughed softly to herself as Amanda cursed under her breath and nursed the burn.

Silver, Marco said as he glanced in Katja's direction. *I imagine those were meant to keep me in line.*

Amanda reached down and picked up a scrap of what remained of her shirt from the floor. Using the material as a barrier, she lifted the cuffs from their post. *I suppose it's fitting, then.*

Katja's eyes widened as she shook her head frantically "no" at Amanda's approach. *"Nein, bitte, ich flehe dich zu stoppen,"* Katja shouted.

"I don't speak German, Katja."

She is begging you to stop.

Amanda blew out a long breath. "Unlike you, Katja, I am not a heartless bitch." Tears of relief slipped from Katja's eyes as Amanda continued. "Although you don't deserve my mercy because you yourself gave none. You *will* wear the cuffs because we cannot trust you, but I will grant you one small token of leniency." She handed Katja two scraps of material. "Wrap this around your wrist to protect your skin. It is the best that I'm willing to do. Be thankful for that."

Amanda clamped the cuffs around Katja's wrists and then tugged her to the cage, locking the other end of the chain to a loop on the cage.

Katja sat on the floor and leaned her back against the wall. "What are you going to do to me?"

Amanda grunted at the question as she walked to Katja's closet. Throwing open the doors, she said, "You should have thought about that before you attacked us." She pulled out a long t-shirt dress and slipped it over her head, then smoothed it over her curves. "I don't imagine you have an objection to me taking this?"

Katja glared back at Amanda, then raised her chin a notch. "I think asking your intentions is a fair question."

Amanda crossed her arms over her chest. "Fair...." She glanced at Marco and noticed he was shifting back. "Tell me, was it 'fair' of *you* to put us through what you did?" Katja sputtered. "Some leader you've turned out to be. You are concerned only for yourself. Not once have you asked about your pack's welfare." Amanda stepped into Marco's embrace. "You are pathetic."

Katja clenched her jaw as her eyes narrowed on Amanda. "Please."

Marco kissed Amanda's forehead as he tightened his embrace. *I liked the view better without the dress.*

She smiled, looking up at him. *I didn't see any clothes in that closet that would fit you.*

He winked down at her. *I will make do.*

Marco turned his head and glared down at Katja. "You and your people will be tried by the council of elders for treason," he said.

~*~

Amanda reached down and plucked the ringing cell phone from the pocket of her shredded jeans. After reading the caller ID, she handed it to Marco. "It's Rafael."

He took the phone. "Rafael.... *Sì,* she is fine.... Tell Caroline that we are not sure...." Marco grunted. "They still live. I hear Clara harping in the background. Tell her that Alessandra would have made her proud." He winked at Amanda. "*Sì,* the situation has been contained for now.... She did?" His smile grew. "I will have to thank her.... *Sì, sì,* we will be waiting." He pressed the end button and handed her back her phone.

Amanda sat down on the edge of the bed. "You will have to thank who?"

Marco chucked her under the chin, then kissed the tip of her nose. "You."

The corners of her mouth turned up in a smile. "What have I done?"

"Rafael said that you packed me a bag of clothes. Thank you, tesoro. It will serve me much better than this sheet."

Amanda's smile grew. "Oh, that. It was no trouble at all. I just packed you one of those fancy suit and tie outfits you are so fond of wearing."

The smile fell from Marco's face. "Suit and tie?"

Amanda lost it in a fit of giggles. "No, *Amante*, I wouldn't do that to you. I packed you a pair of jeans and a t-shirt."

Katja rolled her eyes, burying her face in her hand. "God deliver me," she groaned. "This is sickening to watch."

Marco reached over, took Amanda by the waist, and drug her across his lap, then covered her mouth with his, effectively silencing her laughter. As his tongue slid over hers, Amanda felt his cock harden beneath her.

Amanda broke the kiss, then looked into his eyes. *You are a wicked man.*

I am just a man who desires his mate.

Wicked, I tell you. She wiggled her hips. *We are not alone, and you tease me.*

He growled low. *Behave, woman.*

You started this.

And I am going to finish it.

Amanda scrambled from his lap. *Oh, no, you don't.* She motioned over to Katja, sitting by the cage. *I'm not into that kind of kinky stuff.*

He laughed softly. *Come here, woman.*

She smiled, shaking her head. *No.*

Marco tightened the sheet around his waist and stood up. He reached Amanda in two steps, and sweeping his arm beneath her legs, he threw her, squealing, over his shoulder.

Put me down.

In a moment.

What are you going to do?

Have my wicked way with you, as you put it.

Amanda squirmed in his arms. *Marco.*

He walked through the bathroom door, shutting it behind him. "Now we have privacy," he said as he placed her back on her feet.

"She will hear us."

Marco shrugged. "I do not care." Amanda's eyes widened as she backed up. "She had planned to try to force me into enduring her advances in front of you. 'Try' is the operative word. I would not have allowed it, but her intent was plain."

He pulled her back into his arms, and she felt his cock press into her. "It is time she accepted the fact that I already have a mate." Marco ran his tongue over the vein in her neck and scraped his teeth over the tender spot. Amanda moaned and leaned into him, her body melting into his. "One that I happen to adore." He reached down, pulling at the hem of her dress, tugging it up over her head and dropping it to the floor. Lifting her up, he placed her on the counter and ran his tongue over her pebbled nipple. Amanda threw her head back in abandon, gripping his shoulders with her fingers, and wrapped her legs around his waist as he suckled the nipple deep into his mouth.

Amanda caught her breath, then moaned when Marco ran his fingers over her mound and slipped them into her opening. Her hips rocked toward his hand as his fingers delved deeper.

Marco withdrew his lips and kissed the puckered

peak, his fingers slowing inside her. "Do you still wish for me to stop, *l'amore*?"

Amanda's eyes flew open. "No," came out hoarsely from her mouth. "If you stop now, I might have to hurt you."

He laughed softly, his eyes dark with need. "Tell me what you want."

She placed a hard kiss on his mouth, then looked into his eyes. "I want you to fuck me, *Amante*. I need to feel you between my thighs and fucking me until I don't know where I end and you begin." His smile grew as she continued. "I want to scream out your name as we both cum, and not give a damn *who* hears it."

"I think we can manage that," Marco said as he placed his hands under her hips, lifting her from the counter, then positioning her pussy over his cock. Amanda's mouth devoured his, plunging her tongue inside to war with his as he rolled his hips, sinking deep inside her core. He turned to place her back against the wall for leverage as he withdrew his cock only to impale her again. Amanda matched him stroke for stroke as their bodies moved as one. A primal need took over both of them as the sex grew rougher. She rode his cock hard and fast, her nails leaving jagged lines down his chest and back as she sought mindless release. Amanda howled out his name long and loud as he came with her.

Out of breath, they laughed together as Marco let go of her legs, allowing her feet to again touch the floor.

~*~

Marco turned the shower on and stepped under the spray. "I cannot wait until we get home."

"I can understand that," Amanda said as she followed

him in. "But somehow, I have a feeling you're referring to something very specific." She gazed up into his eyes as she ran the soap over their bodies. His excitement sparked her curiosity. "Why, what do you have in mind?"

"My wolf has seen his mate." She nodded. "He is anxious to run in the woods with her and claim her as his."

"Claim her?"

"Yes."

"How does a wolf lay claim to his mate?"

"He will chase her down in the woods and force her to submit to him."

She shook her head and smiled as she stepped under the water to rinse off. "You don't have to force me to submit to you."

His smile grew. "Your wolf, she will fight it."

"You are teasing me."

"It is in our nature for the female to fight back. It is like a game that arouses us both. He will give chase, and she will try to hide. But once he finds her, he will force her to the ground to submit."

"Submit?"

Marco nodded. "He will mark her as his mate as he fucks her."

Amanda's eyes widened as her wolf responded. "I just felt mine move within me. I believe she is looking forward to it."

"We run as a pack once a month," he said. "You will not believe the freedom you will feel as your paws move swiftly over the soil as you run. There is no other feeling like it."

Amanda kissed his lips, then stepped out of the shower.

"I look forward to experiencing that with you, Amante." After briskly drying her body, she slipped the dress back over her head.

Marco dried off and then looked between the towel and the sheet.

Amanda pointed toward the towel. "I think I'd go with the towel if I were you. You won't trip over it."

"You are probably right. Rafael should be arriving with my bag shortly anyway."

Amanda reached for the doorknob. "Oh yeah? Hmmm, do you think they'll be here soon?"

Marco nodded. "Any time now."

Amanda opened the door and found the room filled with warriors. She stopped in her tracks and looked up at Marco. *Oh, God. Do you think they heard us?*

I am sure they did, judging by the way some are snickering and others won't look me in the eyes.

As Rafael handed Marco his bag, he winked at his alfa. "I figured you might want your clothes."

"Thank you, *sì*," he said as he backed back into the bathroom, closing the door.

Caroline stepped out of the crowd and flung herself at Amanda, hugging her tight. "Girlfriend, I was so worried about you. When I saw you fade and disappear, I was so afraid that something bad had happened to you. Rafael told me that you would be all right, but I needed to see for myself."

"I'm glad to see you too," Amanda said as she hugged her tighter, then she whispered. "Did you hear anything?"

Caroline giggled. "Yes, we all heard quite a bit."

"Oh, my God."

"Don't worry about it. The pack is happy for you both. Rafael told me that not all mated couples enjoy each other as much as you two seem to."

Amanda felt herself flush down to her toes. "Oh, God."

Caroline stepped back. "As I said before, don't worry about it. It is the same between me and Rafael, and I don't care who hears me."

Amanda smiled. "I shouldn't either, I guess. But had I known everyone was here, we would have been more discreet."

Caroline giggled. "But it wouldn't have stopped you."

Amanda laughed with her. "No, I don't suppose it would have."

Marco stepped back into the room and placed his hands on Amanda's shoulders.

She glanced at him and smiled. *I liked the towel.*

He laughed softly and kissed her cheek. *Thank you for packing my bag.*

"Alessandra," Clara said, pulling Amanda into a tight hug.

Amanda's eyes widened. "Nonna—"

Clara stepped back and cupped Amanda's face in her hands. "I am very proud of you."

Amanda laughed nervously. "Okay, what did I do?"

"You have proved to everyone you have what it takes to be our queen." She stepped back, gesturing to the crowd. "You embraced your wolf by tapping into your gifts. Even I didn't know you had the gift of teleportation. There has only been one other with such a gift that I am aware of. But beyond that, you demonstrated restraint and have shown mercy by capturing instead of killing your enemy. Very few can control their wolf and halt the instinct to kill, especially one so new to the shift."

She is right, l'amore. I am proud of you as well.

Clara kneeled before Marco. "*Sono lieto di vedere che tu stia bene, mio re.*"

The warriors stood tall, pounding their chest with their right hand twice in salute to their king. "*Il mio re,*" they shouted in unison.

~*~

Caroline tugged on Rafael's shirt. "What's going on?"

Rafael leaned in to whisper in her ear. "The elder has informed her king of her happiness that he is well. The others are paying tribute to their leader."

Caroline nodded. "What does *Il mio re* mean?"

"My king."

"What would they call Amanda?"

"*La mia regina.*"

"Which is—?"

He laughed softly. "My queen."

She flushed. "Naturally."

"If Marco will allow it, I will teach you everything you need to know."

Caroline looked up at him. "What do you mean by 'allow'?"

Rafael kissed her forehead. "You know how several have referred to you as my mate?" She nodded. "I do want to keep you with me and make it so." Caroline smiled. "But, in order to do so, I need permission from my alfa."

"Why would you need his permission?"

"One reason is I am his enforcer...his right-hand man, so to speak."

"So? I don't see what—"

"There are risks involved, *piccolo*."

"What kind of risks?"

"You would be required to convert."

"Convert?" He nodded. "Like changing my religion or something?"

"No." He winked. "To wolf."

She swallowed hard. "It's dangerous, isn't it?"

"*Sì*, it can be for a weak one, one who is frail and carries a weak life force." Caroline bit her bottom lip as she stared into his eyes. "But you are strong in both will and stature. Your life force shines bright."

"What would I have to give up?"

He let out a long breath. "Your human life. You would no longer be considered a human. You would be converted into a Lycan, like me."

"Lycan?"

"*Sì*, we are children of the moon. Some refer to us as werewolves."

"I may regret this, but I'm going to ask. Exactly how old are you?"

He hesitated. When he had revealed some of his age earlier, she had withdrawn from him. "Does it matter?"

She shrugged. "Not really. I was just trying to figure out how long Lycans really live."

"I am a hundred and twenty-five."

"Wow."

"Our kind fully mature at age twenty-five, and our

bodies do not age after that. That is why the elders look so young. Their ages range, but most are over five hundred."

Caroline did a double-take. "As in years old?"

"*Sì*. Our life spans are eternal. There are a few things that will end our lives, like a silver bullet, a stake to the heart, an attack by an enemy Lycan, or decapitation. Barring any of that happening, we do not die. Sickness and diseases do not plague us." He smiled. "So you see, we would have a very long time to enjoy each other's company."

Caroline smiled in return. "So, how many mates have you had over the years."

"None."

"None?"

He shook his head. "No, we mate for life."

"Amanda said that, but I didn't think she was serious."

"Some mates are bound together by contract, usually arranged by their families. Some are happy, and some are not."

"I bet that kind of situation spawns a lot of infidelity."

Rafael shook his head. "To mess with another's mate is certain death. It is in our genetic makeup to protect what is ours. I am very surprised that our queen was able to overcome the desire to destroy Katja. Both males and females will kill for less than she did to our alfa. I was fortunate in that I was left with the choice to choose the one I desired."

"Me?"

"Yes, *piccolo*."

~*~

Amanda elbowed Marco. "I have been watching Caroline and Rafael."

"So have I."

Amanda looked up at him. "Well, have you been listening too?"

"I have."

"Well?"

Marco raised an eyebrow. "Well what?"

"She has confessed to me that Rafael makes her happy. I heard him explain the risks to her—"

"So?"

"Marco—"

He threw his head back and laughed. "I am teasing you, *tesoro*. I will approve. Rafael," Marco said loudly to get his attention. "Yes, you may."

CHAPTER SEVENTEEN

"If their fate is the elder's decision, I don't see why we have to be present for the verdict," Amanda said as Marco urged her through the door.

Everyone stood and gave silent tribute as they walked by.

Marco nodded to the crowd before he answered her. "Because we are the accusers."

"So?"

"It is our right to stand in witness to their fate," he said as he held out the chair for her.

Amanda plopped down in the seat and glared at him. "I still don't like this."

When Marco sat down next to her, everyone else sat down as well. "This is something that comes with your position as our queen. You will be called upon from time to time to sit in judgment of others."

Amanda threw out her hand. "I do not like to judge others."

Marco smiled. "That in itself will make you fair. Any leader who enjoys wielding power is usually corrupt."

She sighed heavily, then looked out into the crowd. "I never really looked at it from that perspective before. Although I still don't like this, I can see your point."

"Good. We will discuss this later if you still feel the need. The accused are filing in, and we need to remain silent."

The six elders sat at a table in the center of the large meeting room facing the crowd. The accused filed past them into a holding area and took their seats. Clara struck a gavel three times against the wooden sound block on the table, a signal for the accused to rise. There were fifty-five in all. Katja stood to the front as their leader.

Adolfo rose from his seat next to Clara. "We have all heard your sides of the story. We are also aware that most of you were only following the orders given to you by your alfa, Katja, and her second-in-command, Hector. From this day forward, you will no longer follow orders from these two. Katja, you are hereby stripped of your status as the pack's alfa, and Hector, you no longer hold any command. Any of you caught following orders from these two will be put to immediate death."

"What?" Katja shouted as she looked frantically to her pack for support. None would meet her gaze.

Adolfo gestured to the audience. "Raul."

Raul stood. "*Sì, Adolfo anziano.*"

"You are a trusted warrior and, so far, have been unmated. I will trust you to keep Katja Wolf in line. You will be granted enforcer status, but in no way will you allow that one to wield any power." Raul nodded. "She now belongs to you. See that she behaves."

"You cannot do this to me," Katja shouted again.

"We can, and I just did," Adolfo said calmly. "You, young woman, are fortunate we did not condemn you to death for your actions against our king."

Raul inclined his head. "I will do as I am commanded, *Adolfo anziano.*"

"Unbelievable," Katja grumbled as she plopped back down in her chair.

Adolfo gestured to the audience again. "Catjetan."

Catjetan stood. "*Sì, Adolfo anziano.*"

"You are hereby appointed to the position as the new pack alfa."

Catjetan nodded. "I, too, will do as I am commanded, *Adolfo anziano, grazie.*"

Adolfo smiled. "Very well, we will send your mate, Drina, to you as soon as you get things settled here."

"*Grazie, Adolfo*, I am sure she will be pleased."

"As she should be."

~*~

"The elders made good choices," Marco said as they stood up to leave.

"But that doesn't seem fair to Raul...he wasn't given a choice," Amanda said.

Marco smiled. "He wasn't?"

Amanda shook her head. "No, I didn't hear Adolfo give him any choices, just commands."

Marco pointed in Raul's direction. "Look at him, *tesoro*; does he appear to be unhappy with the ruling?"

She saw Raul laughing with his friends, and they were all slapping him on the back, congratulating him. "No, he doesn't."

Marco guided her from the room with his hand on the small of her back. "Since he was not the accused, he could have voiced his objections, and Adolfo would have named another. Raul is suited well for the position of the new pack enforcer. He is not manipulated easily and is very loyal. His new mate will not be able to twist him to her will, and she will have to learn her place."

"I somehow feel sorry for Katja," Amanda said under her breath.

"Why?"

She shrugged. "To be forced into a marriage—"

Marco laughed softly. "Are you feeling sorry for yourself, *l'amore*?"

"Me?" He nodded. "No, why?"

"You were not given any choices either."

She opened her mouth to object, then laughed with him. "I see your point."

"Do not feel sorry for her, Amanda. She will learn her new position within the pack, and once she does, there is room for happiness if she allows herself to experience it. Raul is a good man, and he would not mistreat her."

"What about her old enforcer?"

"Hector?" She nodded for him to continue. "He is not like Raul in the least. Her old enforcer, Hector, will have to be closely watched. He has a mean sadistic streak, and one such as him will not take a demotion lightly. I have a feeling that that one will be causing Catjetan and Raul problems."

She stopped in her tracks and looked up at him, dumbfounded. "So, we'll just abandon them like sitting ducks?"

He shook his head, urging her forward again. "No, not at all. The elders will appoint a force of around ten to leave behind for a time to make sure that order remains. Once the time is up, each of the men will be given a choice to remain here or to return home."

"You must think that I'm a worrywart."

"I told you before that I find your innocence refreshing," he said as he opened the door to the room they were assigned.

She looked around the room as she walked through the door. "Speaking of going home, when can we do that?"

Marco blew out a long breath as he closed the door behind them. "Since the elders will remain behind for a short time, there are two things that must be taken care of here before we go."

Amanda sat down on the edge of the bed, looking up at him. "What two things? I will be honest. I am ready to return home. I only brought us a single change of clothes."

"Our part requires no clothing."

Amanda stared, waiting for him to continue. He did not.

She jumped up from the edge of the bed and started to pace. "Oh, no, you don't, mister. You cannot clam up on me now." She stopped and jabbed her forefinger at his chest. "You are implying that I'm going to have to do something naked, and I need to know right now what that something is."

"Our coronation."

She shook her head no frantically, backing up. "If you think I am going to stand in front of our pack naked and have everyone gawking at me to receive a crown...." Amanda crossed her arms stubbornly across her chest. "You better think again."

"There are no official crowns, *l'amore*."

She snorted, throwing out her arms. "Like that makes much of a difference," she said, then resumed pacing.

Marco walked up behind her and placed his hands on her shoulders, halting her tirade. "It is true, we will not be wearing any clothing," he said softly, "but we will be standing before the pack and elders as our wolves, not in human form."

"You know you just made me feel like a total idiot, *Amante*." He laughed softly. "Why didn't you just say that to begin with?"

He laughed harder. "You've been so full of pent-up frustrations today that I felt you needed to expel a little of it."

She laughed with him. "Okay. When are we supposed to do this?"

"Tonight."

"Okay, tonight, that is fine. What is the other thing we have to do?"

"As you know, I have given Rafael permission to take Caroline as his mate."

Amanda sat back down on the edge of the bed, and Marco joined her. "Yes."

"Since we do not know how long it will be before the elders return to Chicago, Rafael will convert her this afternoon, before our coronation."

Amanda frowned. "He's going to hurt her."

"In theory, yes, but she does not have to feel the pain." Marco brushed a stray hair away from her face. "As the queen, you can compel her."

"I've never done that before."

Marco shrugged. "Since you have transcended, you should have all of your powers now. If you can teleport from an airplane to here, compelling someone should be a simple task."

"No pressure there."

"If it will make you feel better, we will test it first."

"On who?"

"Caroline."

"How?"

"Just simply compel her to do something she would not normally do."

Amanda looked up when there was a knock at the door. "I wonder who that is?"

Marco smiled. "That would be Rafael and Caroline."

"Wow, that's some timing."

Marco smiled. "No, not really. I sent Rafael a text to his cell phone when you were sitting there feeling sorry for Raul and Katja."

Amanda smacked him on the arm, laughing. "Oh, you!"

"Come in," Marco said loudly.

Rafael opened the door and let Caroline precede him into the room. They were both dressed in long red velvet robes.

Amanda rose from the edge of the bed and greeted her friend with a hug. "Are you sure this is what you want, baby girl?" Amanda whispered.

Caroline pulled back and smiled. "Yes."

"We have been over this thoroughly, my queen. I have made sure she knows what to expect," Rafael said.

"Caroline," Amanda said. "I've been told that the conversion of a human to a wolf is painful."

Caroline took a shaky breath and nodded. "I will bear it."

Amanda took her hands in hers. "Marco has told me it is within my power to compel you to not feel any pain."

"Can you do that?"

"He says I can, so I wanted to test it first in here."

"What are you going to do?"

"I will compel you to do something you wouldn't normally do on your own, and I will tell you not to remember it. If it works in here, it should work out there, in theory." Amanda squeezed her hands. "Are you willing to try it?"

Caroline smiled. "Yes."

Amanda shook her hands out and stood straighter, then gazed into Caroline's eyes. "You will walk across the floor twice, once in each direction, walking and clucking like a chicken." Both Marco and Rafael laughed out loud. Amanda kept eye contact with Caroline and motioned for them to stop laughing. "When you have completed your walk, you will go up to Rafael and kiss him. When I say the word baby girl, you will begin."

She is not going to be happy with you, l'amore.

I couldn't think of anything else to tell her to do.

Amanda looked away.

"When are you going to begin?" Caroline asked.

Amanda smiled. "Any moment, baby girl—"

Caroline's eyes glazed over, and she stood up straight. Then she started bobbing her head, clucking as she made her way across the floor. She did exactly what she was told and ended it with kissing Rafael. She turned back toward Amanda and shook her head. "Well, when are you going to begin?"

Caroline flushed when everyone started laughing; she looked down at herself and spread her arms wide. "Amanda, what did you make me do?"

Amanda gave her a hug. "You truly don't remember?"

"No."

She let go and stepped away from Caroline. "Then, I guess I can compel you."

Caroline crossed her arms over her chest. "No, really, Mandy, what did you compel me to do?"

"Promise you won't be mad?"

"That bad, huh?"

Amanda laughed. "No, but it would be embarrassing."

"Whatever, just tell me."

"Do you remember the chicken joke we used to do at sleepovers in middle school?"

"You had me clucking like a chicken?"

"You were a beautiful chicken," Rafael said between laughs.

Caroline covered her face with her hands and laughed. "I guess it could have been worse. And yes, you were right. I wouldn't have done that on my own."

Rafael stood up and straightened his robe. "It is almost time to go."

Caroline gripped Amanda's hand in a panic. "What do we do?"

CHAPTER EIGHTEEN

"It is not very often that one of us chooses to take a human for a mate," Clara said formally. "However, our alfa's enforcer, Rafael, has chosen to do just that. His human, Caroline, has accepted him and will be initiated into our pack to be witnessed by all." She spread her arm wide and stepped to the side.

The warriors pounded on their chest twice in salute as Rafael and Caroline walked hand in hand to the front of the group.

Rafael whispered, "Just try to relax, *piccolo*."

She squeezed his hand and continued to look straight ahead. "I will be fine."

"You don't look fine. You look scared to death.... *Piccolo*, you don't have to go through with this. I understand."

"No...I—" She glanced his way, giving him a weak smile. "I really do want this. Maybe a little bit of that chicken wore off on me." Rafael smiled. "It'll all be over shortly, and I'll be one of you. Piece of cake, right?"

"In theory—"

"Great, you could have gone all day without saying

that."

"I was a small child when I witnessed this ceremony. I have not participated in it myself."

She took a ragged breath and smiled. "Just try not to kill me, huh?"

"Never."

"I'm going to hold you to that."

They stopped and stood before Marco and Amanda and then dropped to their knees.

"I am proud to accept a new member into our pack," Marco said. "Caroline has demonstrated her loyalty and has shown great courage. She already has the heart of a wolf. Rafael has chosen well. You may both rise and face each other."

As the couple rose to their feet to face each other, they let the robes slide from their shoulders to pool at their feet. "Caroline," Marco continued, "You have been instructed in our ways. You must confess to all that you understand that by choosing Rafael, you are choosing to irreversibly change your human life as you now know it to become a Lycan." She nodded. "Once you confess, I will call forth Rafael's wolf, and you will become one of us."

"I understand."

"Very well, then turn to the pack and confess."

Amanda whispered, "It'll be okay, baby girl," as Caroline faced the pack.

As Caroline spread her arms wide, Marco braced one arm, and Amanda braced the other. Caroline took a ragged breath before she spoke. "I, Caroline Robinson, confess to you all that I understand the risks and consequences of my decision to accept Rafael as my mate. The pack is now my family and will remain so for eternity." She raised her chin a notch. "Of my own free will, I accept you, Rafael Acardi, as my mate and all that comes with it."

Marco had explained to Amanda earlier that not all Lycans could shift at will without the aid of the full moon or intense anger. An alfa possessed the ability to force a pack member or the entire pack to shift with just a command. When an alfa ordered the shift, it was an immediate and sometimes painful response, as opposed to the normal gradual contortion of the body.

"Rafael, your new mate calls to you," Marco said. "As your alfa, I command you, shift and claim her."

Amanda gripped Caroline's arm tighter as Rafael's wolf burst forth. She felt Caroline's arm tremble beneath her fingers as the large wolf towered over her. Rafael was nearly as large as his alfa. "Close your eyes and accept him, baby girl. You will remember everything, but you will feel no pain. Do not fear him."

Caroline smiled at Rafael. "I will hold you to your promise."

Rafael nodded, then threw back his massive head and howled. Behind him, the pack howled in response. He lowered his head and slowly, almost reverently, licked across her torso. Baring his teeth, he bit her side deep. The flesh tore as he let go and gripped again. Marco and Amanda held tighter to support Caroline's weight as her knees buckled and she lost consciousness.

Marco, he's killing her.

No, tesoro, she will survive. He must bring her almost to the point of death and pour his essence into her. It is dangerous, but she is strong.

Caroline's body started to shake. *She's convulsing, is that supposed to happen?*

Yes, death is near. Please remain calm and help me lower her to the ground. His grip must remain tight until the transfer is complete, and we don't want him to tear into her any more than necessary.

Amanda helped Marco ease her friend to the ground. She knelt beside her and cradled Caroline's head on her lap, brushing the sweat-soaked hair away from Caroline's face. She was very pale but showed no signs of physical pain.

Rafael released his grip and licked the wound closed. Although Caroline remained unconscious, the tension left her body.

Amanda brushed her fingers across Caroline's face again. "Now what?" she said softly and looked up at Marco.

Rafael shifted back and kneeled down, placing Caroline's robe over her nude body. He took her from Amanda and cradled her close to his body, rocking her as he would a child.

"We wait," Marco said as he helped Amanda to her feet.

~*~

Amanda stepped out of the side door of their room and stood at the edge of the woods. The full moon illuminated the area in a pale glow, outlining a few animals along the woods' perimeter who were curious enough to investigate her presence. For the first time in her life, she felt at one with nature. She smiled when the wind kicked up, sending her red velvet robe flapping around her bare legs. Raising her chin, she sniffed the air; the woods were alive, and her wolf was getting antsy.

Marco walked up behind her, pulling her back against his body in a tight embrace. "Have I told you lately how beautiful you are?"

Amanda leaned into him. "You have." She turned in his arms and placed her cheek on his chest. "But I don't think I'll ever tire of hearing you say it."

He laughed softly. "What are you doing?"

"My wolf is restless." She looked up into his eyes. "I figured I'd come out here and appease her for a bit before the ceremonies."

"She will not be happy until you allow her out to run."

"I can sense that from her as well, but she'll have to be patient a bit longer. We have obligations, and then we have to come back and pack. I am ready to return home. My apartment is a wreck."

Marco nodded. "I will have your things moved into the unit I have been living in."

"But I like my apartment, Marco."

"The entire building belongs to us, *l'amore*. I can have a crew come in and combine both units together, and we can have the entire top floor. Or, if you wish, we can move into any number of properties we now own together. The point is, I want us to be happy, and I really do not care where we live as long as it is together."

"Together," she said wistfully. "After all I just went through to get you back, I'll have to agree. Hmmm...my apartment has been reduced to rubble. I like your apartment too. A larger unit would be nice."

Smiling, he held her tighter. "*Our* apartment. What belongs to me now belongs to you as well."

She returned his smile. "Okay, okay, I'm still getting used to all this. *Our* apartment." She frowned when she'd had a moment to absorb what he said. "Wait a minute. Any number of properties?" He nodded. "Just how many properties do *we* own?"

"Twenty-one, including the apartment building, counting it as a whole, not adding the units individually. We own three nightclubs, an attorney's office, and now an advertising agency. The rest are houses with acreage on or near our pack land."

Her eyes widened. "You're an attorney too?"

"No. A couple of our pack members are. They work for us."

"Wow, you have created quite an empire for yourself."

"I have had the last three hundred years to do it. Of course, the names have changed on the deeds over the years to look like the properties have been passed down through the generations. That is one of the things we use the attorneys for—to keep our existence a secret. Most of us have been successful in keeping our secret, but as you may have guessed, a few have not."

"The myths?"

"*Sì*, a careless move on our part and stories surface. We can control our beasts, and we do not hunt and kill humans unless it is to protect our secret. A human's fear of the unknown and an overactive imagination put our kind in danger if we are discovered. We are the superior race, but we are no match for a human army equipped with bombs and silver."

"No, I guess not."

She turned in Marco's arms to face the woods again and leaned into him, letting out a long sigh. "It is beautiful here."

"It is.... I can't wait to show you the view from one of the houses. It is spectacular, and the hunting is excellent."

"Hunting...." She laughed. "I've never hunted a day in my life. Picking up a gun and shooting an innocent creature has never much appealed to me."

Marco kissed her cheek, laughing softly with her. "You will have no need for a gun, *tesoro*. Your wolf will be the one to crave the hunt. The chase is exhilarating."

"That is something I'll have to take your word for."

"You will find out soon enough. We will be running together very soon." He squeezed tighter. "My wolf is looking forward to giving chase to yours. He fights me even now to be released and dominate you."

"Dominate...I'm not really sure I like the sound of that."

"The cat and mouse game we play is exciting to us both. Your wolf will run, and when she is caught, she will fight mine."

"You told me earlier that my wolf would fight yours, and yours would force mine to submit." She looked up at him when he nodded. "What did you mean by that?"

"He will force her down to the ground and fuck her, claiming her as his mate, and he will mark her as his."

Amanda felt her wolf move beneath her skin. She

remembered how large Marco's wolf was, and the prospect both excited her and scared the hell out of her at the same time. "I felt her move."

"She wishes to be set free. It is time to go. Are you ready to shift?"

She stepped out of his arms and shrugged. "I've never shifted at will before. The other two times were out of anger."

"Soon, it will become second nature to you. Remove your robe and place it by our door." Marco said as he removed his own robe. "We will need them when we return." She nodded and dropped her robe next to his. "Now, take a deep breath and try to will her forward."

Amanda blew out a breath while she shook the tension out of her hands, then she balled her hands into fists and strained, making a face as she did so.

Marco threw back his head and laughed. "What are you doing?"

"Don't laugh at me, damn it. I'm just doing what you told me to do."

Marco laughed harder. "I did not tell you to do that. I told you to will her forward, not push—"

"Damn it, I said to stop laughing," came out in a snarl as her wolf sprung toward him. His shift was instant as her wolf took him to the ground, where they rolled over a couple of times. His wolf came out on top. She snapped her jaws at him in an attempt to throw him off. *Get off me, asshole.*

Tu sei bella quando sei arrabbiato, tesoro.

I'm pissed off at you right now. Stop trying to flatter me by telling me that I'm beautiful when I'm angry. I know better than that. Her wolf struggled again. *Now get off me.*

Marco nuzzled her throat, then licked her muzzle.

Amanda growled low. *Stop that.*

His wolf snorted. *It is time for us to go.* He stepped off her and let her rise. *I am looking forward to picking this back up at a later time.*

There won't be a later time, she huffed.

~*~

The field was beautiful beneath the soft glow of the full moon, Amanda noticed as she approached. A soft breeze was blowing through the tall grasses, adding to the melody of the crickets and bullfrogs. Fireflies dotted the night sky and danced along the edges of the forests. As she and Marco got closer, the pack formed an outer circle with the council of elders in the middle. Two wolves stepped aside to let them pass, then stepped back in line. The entire pack lowered their front shoulders and heads to the ground in obedience to their alfas as they walked by.

Upon looking around, Amanda noticed that Marco was twice the size of the other males, with the exception of his enforcer, Rafael. He was easy to spot due to his massive size. Caroline stood next to her mate. Her shiny white coat stood out in stark contrast to his black one.

Amanda's heart swelled with pride at seeing her friend. *Marco, she is a beautiful wolf.*

Yes, my enforcer has chosen well.

I was worried about her, but now I see she will adapt just fine.

Just as you will, l'amore. You have my heartfelt apologies for laughing at you earlier, but you looked so damn cute with that expression on your face. We will work on teaching you to shift at will when we return home.

It's hard to stay mad at you, Amante.

His wolf snickered. *Amante sounds so much better rolling off your tongue than asshole.*

She turned her head and nipped at his shoulder as they stopped in front of the elders. *Behave.*

The six elders rose in unison and bayed loudly, then stepped aside.

What are they doing, Amante?

They are relinquishing control to us, he said as he motioned for her to step forward. They then turned and faced the pack.

The pack filed by, one by one, bowing and showing allegiance, ending with Rafael and Caroline. The four stood side by side and howled.

The pack bayed in return.

It is done, Marco said.

That wasn't so hard.

He turned his head to look at her, and his wolf snuffled. *Run!*

Amanda took a step back and looked around for danger. *What?*

Rafael and Caroline backed away as Amanda looked around, confused.

His wolf stepped forward, towering over her, forcing her to back up again, and howled. *Run!*

Her heart hammered in her chest as she took off for the woods. She felt the earth turn beneath her feet as her massive paws dug into the soil. The wind soaring past her was exhilarating as she picked up speed. Trees were a blur as she darted and zigzagged between them at full speed. She had never felt more freedom in her life.

Amanda felt rather than heard Marco's pursuit. As she sailed over a felled log, a solid thud knocked the breath from her and took her down as she rolled, fur flying, snapping at her attacker. She regained her feet, backing up, growling low as the hackles raised the fur on her neck.

Marco stepped from the darkness, towering over her. Amanda turned to run again when he pounced on her, taking her to the ground and pinning her front shoulders down. When she turned her head to snap at him, he bit down on her shoulder, ripping into the muscle until she stilled.

As she used her hind legs, attempting to stand, his cock entered her hard and fast. Amanda felt her wolf moan in response. She brought her hips up to meet each powerful thrust as he drove his cock in and out, filling and stretching her tight sheath. She felt her world explode as her mate howled out his release.

He released the grip on her shoulder and licked the wound clean as he stood over her. Amanda rolled over onto her back and shifted back to human form. Marco ran his tongue across her cheek.

"That was amazing," she said and propped up on her elbows to look at him. "I love you, *Amante.*"

Marco stood over her as he shifted back. "*Ti amo più,*" he said as he dropped to the ground beside her. "My wolf is sated for a while." He leaned over and ran his tongue across her pert nipple, nipping the tender bud as he fisted his cock and stroked. "But the man is still hungry for his mate."

Amanda rose up on her knees and ran her tongue along the vein in his neck. "We will see what we can do about that. But this time, it is my turn to dominate and take control," she said as she pushed him down on his back. "Lay still, *la mia alfa*, and let me play for a while."

He threw out his hands, smiling up at her. "I am yours to command."

The corners of her mouth turned up in a smile as she reached for his cock. "Mmmmm...it must be love for an alfa to relinquish command."

His smile grew. "Eternal, *il mio piccolo lupo alfa.*"

Amanda ran her fingers lightly over his cock as she looked into his eyes. "Do not cum until I allow it."

Marco swallowed hard, nodding once. "I had not realized you were into torture." Her smile grew. "But you have my word as an alfa."

"I believe you will enjoy yourself, *Amante.*"

"Of that, I have no doubt.... The question that remains is, will I survive it?"

"That remains to be seen," she said, then leaned down and ran her tongue over his cock from base to tip. Amanda swirled her tongue around the base of the crown, then took the purple head into her mouth, suckling as she cupped his balls in the palm of her hand.

Marco caught his breath and surged his cock deeper into her mouth as she took him down her throat. His body shook as her moan vibrated along his cock. "*Buon dio*," he panted as he pitched his hips again, surging deeper down her throat. Wrapping his fingers in her hair, he held her head while she took as much of him as she could as he fucked her mouth.

When she felt he was ready to come, she backed off,

sat up, and straddled his hips. "You cannot cum yet, *Amante*," she said as she gazed into his eyes. Amanda saw the tension of holding back etched into his features, and his body was covered in a light sheen of sweat. Seeing him needy for her like this gave her a new sense of power. She smiled as she rocked her pussy tauntingly over his straining cock. When he gripped her hips, her smile grew. "Uh uh, Amante, *I* am in charge."

"You are a tease," he said, reaching for her breasts.

"But you are enjoying every second of it," she said as she smacked his hands away. "When I am ready, you can have your turn, but until then, the hands need to remain where I can see them."

"Two can play at this game, *la mia alfa*," he said hoarsely.

"I have no doubt you will return the favor," she purred as she rocked her pussy over his cock again. "But for now, I want you to fuck me hard as I ride your cock, and when I tell you to cum, I want to feel you swell and explode inside me."

Marco laughed softly. "My life is eternal, but I swear you will be the death of me." He adjusted his hips and smacked her on the butt. "But if I have to die, to die like this would make me a happy wolf."

She laughed with him. "You won't be dying anytime soon, *Amante*," she said in a teasing tone. "I do, however, want you to be a happy wolf, so make me a happy wolf and use your hands."

He laughed harder. "Is there something you want in particular?"

She nodded. "This is a new position for me. Although the concept is rather simplistic, it is a little awkward."

He held his cock for her. "Will this help?"

"Yes." She rose up on her knees and then eased her pussy down over his cock.

Marco reached up and pulled her face down to his, devouring her mouth. When he let go, he said. "Don't ever change, *piccolo*."

"*Ti amo, Marco*," she said as he placed his hands on her hips and helped her obtain a rhythm. His hips rose to meet her every stroke. Taking him in deeper and harder than she ever had before, Amanda rode him with abandon, letting go of her inhibitions and allowing the pure sensation to flow over her. As she reached her peak, she yelled, "Cum for me, *Amante*." He surged his hips one more time and took both of them over the edge.

CHAPTER NINETEEN

Amanda stepped through the opening on the plane and looked inside. Other than a couple toward the back, the plane was empty. That bothered her. It was going to be a very long flight home, and she was ready to get it over with. She looked over her shoulder at Marco, coming up behind her. "We must be early."

Marco glanced in her direction as he stowed their bags in an overhead compartment. "No, in fact, we are running a little late."

Stopping in her tracks, she turned around to face him. "Late?"

"*Sì*, we were supposed to take off twenty minutes ago."

"Why didn't you say anything earlier?"

Marco flashed her a smile. "I was a bit preoccupied." He sent her mental images of them together that morning, having sex in the bed, on the floor, and then again in the shower.

The room suddenly felt hot, and Amanda flushed as the images raced through her head. They left her feeling aroused and needy. If it took her a hundred years, she was going to figure out how he did that and return the favor.

Winking at her, he continued. "Other than causing the pilot an inconvenience with the flight plan, our lateness is of little importance. The plane belongs to us."

Clearing her throat, she said, "You will pay for that one, *Amante*."

His smile grew. "At least you are still calling me by my pet name."

"Asshole did cross my mind."

He threw back his head and laughed. "You are a treasure." He lowered his voice and said, "I will make it up to you when we get back home."

She smirked. "I'm sure you will try." She looked around the plane again. "If we are so late, where are the others?"

"The two in the back are Rafael and Caroline. It will just be the four of us."

She turned her head again, frowning. "I could have sworn I distinctly heard several men talking about returning home today. Why are they not flying with us?" She looked past Marco when the flight attendant secured the door.

"You know how much stock Lycans put into superstition and prophecy."

She shrugged, then continued to walk down the aisle. "Yeah, so?"

"They do not want to fly with you."

Amanda stopped in her tracks, and Marco bumped into her. "Why, what did I do?"

He urged her forward again. "They had never seen anyone teleport before."

She snorted, "Neither had I. So?"

"In our history, there had only been one other with that ability. Although they do not fear you, it will be some time before any will voluntarily step on a plane with you again."

"At least I see Caroline and Rafael still love me."

"We do," Caroline said as she rose from the chair and embraced Amanda.

"The pack loves you, *tesoro*...they would give their lives for you," Marco said as they sat down. "They know you are still learning what your abilities are and do not know what to expect. I guess they are afraid of getting caught in the crossfire, so to speak. Give them a little time."

Amanda felt the plane begin its taxi down the runway. She loved to fly but always hated the takeoff. "Whatever," Amanda said under her breath, then smiled at Caroline, attempting to put her mind on something else. "You look happy, baby girl. How are you feeling?"

"Overwhelmed?" she said and giggled. "Now I know what you were going through. These mood swings are going to take some getting used to."

"That part doesn't last," Rafael said as he took Caroline's hand in his. "Once your body has adjusted to the new changes, you will not suffer through the mood swings anymore."

Caroline blew out a breath. "All I can say is Charlie better watch himself around me now. I might literally bite his head off."

Laughing, Amanda nodded in agreement. "I nearly did that the morning before I met Marco for the first time."

"I remember that," Caroline said, laughing with her. "Now that I know what you were feeling, I'm surprised you didn't. You were just plain scary that day. I find myself being pissy with Rafael for no reason." She glanced at Rafael and winked as she continued speaking to Amanda. "Luckily for me, he just laughs and doesn't take it personally. That must have been scary for you, feeling like this and not knowing what was going on with your body."

Marco sat back in the chair, casually extending his legs and crossing his feet. "For the most part, Amanda has adapted well," he said to Caroline. "You will too. Since you were human, it may take you a little longer to adjust, but you have Rafael to help you through it. Being mates, you cannot permanently harm the other, so do not be afraid to be yourself when you are together. Rafael can handle anything you dish out."

Rafael squeezed Caroline's fingers until she looked at him. "I look forward to every day we spend together," he said, then winked at her. "Even the days that might not seem to be going well for you."

"But I feel like I've been such a bitch to you."

Rafael laughed, then leaned over and kissed her cheek. "It is the changes in your body. Soon you will be back to the loveable you that stole my heart."

Caroline sniffed and wiped a tear from her cheek. "Now, I really feel guilty. You're being too nice to me."

Laughing, Amanda said, "He's being a man, girlfriend. He knows you're hormonal right now. Here's the translation." She lowered her voice an octave. "'Babe, I know you're being a bitch, but I still love you. Can we still get naked together later?'"

When Rafael looked to Marco for help, Caroline

laughed. "Oh, you are so busted, handsome."

Rafael looked at the group in confusion. "I will never understand women," Rafael said.

Marco smiled. "He speaks from the heart, ladies." He gestured to Rafael. "We wolves are unlike human males. Since we mate for life, we do not have a need for ulterior motives. Mates can feel what the other feels, so if Caroline reaches out, she will discover that his words are sincere. But if you still feel that you need words, Caroline, he does indeed love and respect you. He is not in it solely for sex like my sweet mate just implied. Since you were a human, taking you for a mate was not a decision to be taken lightly. In fact, it is rarely done. He has already accepted you for who you are, the good and the bad."

"Now I *am* going to cry," Caroline said as Amanda rolled her eyes.

"I will be glad when your hormones are under control," Amanda said. "You switching from crying to laughing to crying again reminds me of a pregnant woman—" Her eyes widened as she thought about it. She looked at Marco. "That's not possible, is it?"

"*Sì*, they are mates."

"Hello, people, I'm right here," Caroline said. "Stop talking around me like I'm not. There is no way that I'm pregnant."

"I mean, it would be too soon to know, right?" Amanda continued. "They just met."

"Amanda—"

Amanda held up her hand to Caroline, waiting on Marco's reply.

"We know from the moment it happens," he said. "Rafael would know if his mate has conceived. Her scent will have changed to him."

They all turned to Rafael.

Caroline swallowed hard before she spoke. "Well, handsome? Please tell me that I still smell the same and that Mandy has lost her mind."

Rafael reached out, caressing Caroline's cheek with the back of his fingers, then nodded once. "You carry my pups, *piccolo*."

Caroline sat back in her chair, blinking in confusion. "I don't understand. I've known you less than a week."

Amanda's mouth dropped open. "Did you say 'pups' as in plural?"

Rafael smiled proudly. "*Sì*, she will gift me with two fine sons."

Amanda looked at Marco. "It appears you have left out a little in your explanation of things to me."

Marco smiled. "You want to know how this happens?" She nodded. "Well, I thought you knew, but it starts with sex between—"

Amanda smacked his arm, and both he and Rafael laughed. "I know how a woman gets pregnant, ass—" She took a deep breath and continued. "You're baiting me, and I know you two find this highly amusing, but Caroline and I need to know how all this works."

"As I was saying, the male plants the seed—"

"Marco!" Amanda snapped. "Be serious. A baby is a life-changing event. Caroline still has to get used to the idea, and she only has nine months to plan—" Marco shook his head no. "She doesn't have nine months?"

"No, *l'amore*, *you* only have six weeks."

Amanda and Caroline exchanged glances. "What do you mean *I* only have six weeks? We were talking about Caroline, not me...." Amanda's eyes widened when he shook his head no again. "You were referring to me?"

"You both, actually. You conceived that first night I claimed you as my mate."

Amanda sputtered. "And just when were you planning on telling me?"

Marco shrugged. "I thought you knew. Normally a female wolf can sense these things as soon as her mate does."

"Geez, Marco, there has been nothing normal about me from day one. Everything about me being a wolf was wiped from my memories and is just now slowly coming back to me. Do not assume that I know things, especially something this important."

"You carry my pups, *tesoro*, one of each." He smiled as Amanda sat back in her seat, staring at him. "You'll bear my son from the prophecy and a daughter who I hope has her mother's beauty and spirit."

Amanda glanced over at Caroline, who looked as overwhelmed as she felt. "I don't know if I'm ready to be a mother, Marco."

"Nor I a father, but together we will adapt, *l'amore*. You were born to be mine and bear us a son."

"But so soon? I figured that we'd have more time together as a couple."

"We will have eternity to be together as a couple. When I introduce you to the rest of the pack, I want you to take a look at the families. You will notice that there are only one to three pups within a family unit. Since our lives are eternal, the women only conceive once every twenty-five years, once to each new generation. It is built into our genetics. And again, we only repeat that cycle for about five generations. Otherwise, we would overpopulate the earth."

"You say I only have six weeks?"

He shrugged. "Give or take. I believe it's actually closer to five."

Amanda sat up straight in her seat and looked over at Caroline. "We have some major shopping to do, girlfriend."

CHAPTER TWENTY

Marco lifted Amanda out of her seat and carried her to the car. She and Caroline had talked for hours, planning the nurseries and what they would actually tell people at work. Marco told them they could compel people to believe anything they wanted them to, but the women remained skeptical and worried over the details. They had both fallen into an exhausted sleep about an hour before the plane landed in Chicago.

Amanda felt the night air blowing across her arms and opened her eyes just as they reached the car.

"We're almost home," Marco said softly.

She yawned. "I'm glad we've landed." She stretched when he placed her on her feet. "That is a long flight."

Marco opened the back door for Rafael to place his sleeping mate on the seat. He crawled into the back and cuddled her into his lap. "*Sì*, it is," he said as he shut the door. "I am happy we have this day to rest before we have to go back into the office tomorrow."

"It's Sunday already?"

"*Sì*, it's about one a.m."

"No wonder I'm tired. You must be too. It has been a trying weekend."

He embraced her in a hug, breathing in her scent as he kissed the top of her head. "Some moments were trying, but others I will never forget."

He stepped away from Amanda and opened the front passenger door for her. She smiled up at him as she slid onto the seat. "*Grazie.*"

"*Di niente.*"

Amanda watched him walk around the front of the car to the driver's side. She felt the same tingle in her stomach and still had a difficult time believing that he actually belonged to her. He sensed her thoughts and smiled at her as he slid into the driver's seat and shut the door.

I look at you and feel the same wonder, l'amore, he said as he started the engine.

At times I still feel that this is all a dream that started that night you left the basket for me at work, and I will wake up on my couch with a half-empty bottle of wine on the coffee table. You are not a dream, are you?

He laughed softly as he turned down the dirt road. *No, tesoro, you are not dreaming.*

Are you dropping them off at Caroline's apartment?

No, my unit has four bedrooms...they will remain with us for the night. Once everyone has rested, we have things to discuss as a group.

~*~

Amanda rolled over and felt Marco pull her back to the warmth of his body. He was spooned behind her, keeping her close with his arm draped around her waist and his head on her shoulder. When she rolled to her back, he moved his head to lay it on her chest and tightened his grip.

While gazing at his profile, she marveled that in his sleep, he could appear to be so innocent, especially when she knew he was anything but. She ran the back of her hand affectionately over his stubble. He opened his eyes and looked up at her.

"Good morning, *Amante.*"

He smiled. "Good morning." He brought his hand up to rub the stubble on his cheek and frowned. "I need to shave."

"You do." She laughed. "But you have a good excuse. I was more concerned with bringing you clothes than toiletries when I was packing. Rafael teased me for bringing two bags as it was."

He kissed her belly before he sat up. "I can hear them in the kitchen."

"Mmmm, it smells like Caroline has found your coffee." Amanda paused and looked at him. "Wait a minute. The cabinets and refrigerator were empty when we left."

"They were," Marco said as he slid his legs over the side of the bed. "Clara called ahead and told the pack members to have the apartment ready for our return."

She propped up on her elbows and looked around. "That was thoughtful of her."

"There are his and her closets in here. Yours should be filled with your clothes. Some of the drawers in the dresser should hold your clothes as well."

He stood and stretched his muscular body. Amanda bit her lip as she watched him walk away toward the bathroom.

Holy Mary, Mother of God, she thought to herself. *What an ass.*

He laughed softly. "I can hear your thoughts, *tesoro*."

"Good," she said as she slid out of bed. "Know this. As soon as our company is gone, that ass is mine."

As Amanda passed the bathroom, she heard the water running in the sink. She opened the closet door Marco had pointed to and found her things inside color-coded. She pulled out a pair of blue jeans and a t-shirt and laid them across the bed.

Marco stepped up to the doorway as he dried his face. He ran his hand over the smooth skin and smiled. "That feels much better. I am about to step into the shower. Join me?"

"What about our company?"

"It is just going to be a shower, *l'amore*. As you said, we have company, but later—"

She smiled. "Later sounds good." Amanda made her way to him and cupped his face in her hands, bringing her lips to his in a lingering kiss. "That was a little something to make sure you didn't forget about later."

"Keep it up, and we will be taking our shower cold."

~*~

As Amanda towel-dried her hair, the scent of bacon caught her attention. "Caroline must be cooking breakfast," she said to Marco.

"*Sì*, it smells like it," Marco said as he slipped his t-shirt over his head and smoothed it into place. "Are you almost ready?"

She threw the towel in the hamper. "You sure have been secretive," she said, then looked at him.

"No secrets," he shrugged noncommittally. "Just

things we need to talk about as a group."

Crossing her arms over her chest, Amanda leaned her backside against the dresser, giving him a contemplative stare, then smirked. "You know, if I really wanted to, I could dig inside that stubborn head of yours for answers."

"You could," he said, then smiled. "But you won't because there is no need to." He gestured toward the door.

Amanda pushed away from the dresser and walked with him to the kitchen.

Caroline was preparing the last plate when they arrived. Smiling, she turned with the pan and spatula in hand. "Good morning," she said, then turned to load the items into the dishwasher. "Marco, I hope you don't mind. I've made myself at home in your kitchen."

"*La mia casa è la tua casa.*"

Caroline looked at Rafael. "What did he just say?"

Rafael pulled out her chair for her and kissed her on the cheek as she sat down. "He said, 'my house is your house.'"

She smiled as everyone sat down at the table. "Thank you. I guess between you three, I'll eventually learn your language."

Amanda reached over and squeezed her friend's hand. "No, thank *you*. It smells good."

"It does, doesn't it?" Caroline picked up her fork. "You know, since Rafael changed me, my sense of smell is off the charts." She took a bite and cocked her head to the side. "Things taste better too."

"It is your wolf," Rafael said.

"I know what you mean, baby girl," Amanda said as she picked up her coffee cup. "I'm still discovering things new to me."

~*~

"Okay, *Amante*," Amanda said as she sat back in her chair. "We're all finished with breakfast, and you haven't once hinted at this big secret of yours."

Rafael laughed as Marco raised an eyebrow at his mate.

"What?" Marco threw out his hands. "There is no secret, just things that need to be discussed as a group." He leaned forward in his chair and placed his arms on the table. "We need to decide what is going to happen in the next few days."

Amanda frowned. "Your meaning?"

Marco gestured to Rafael. "Rafael has been my enforcer for the last hundred years, and he will remain so."

Amanda shrugged. "Yeah, so?"

"I guess what you did not know is that Rafael has a room here and lives with me."

Amanda looked at Rafael when he nodded. "O-k-a-y," Amanda said slowly. "Are you proposing that he move Caroline in here with us?"

Marco shook his head. "I want to explain something before I propose any solutions."

She shrugged again. "I'm listening."

"I am, too," Caroline said as she frowned at Rafael. "Because I can see it becoming awful crowded in this apartment with two couples and four babies."

Marco nodded as he continued. "I happen to agree with that statement, Caroline. And now that I have my own mate, I, too, would like my privacy. The dilemma lies in that, as my enforcer, Rafael has to be close to me to respond at a moment's notice. Up until now, he has done pretty much whatever I have told him to do. Now, I have some thoughts that I would like to run past you all as a group since my decisions affect every one of you."

"Marco, you are my alfa," Rafael said, then threw his hands out. "It is my duty to abide by your decisions."

"It is, Rafael, and I appreciate your loyalty, but in this instance, as my enforcer, I want your honest opinion."

"Okay."

Marco sat back in his chair and gestured to the room at large. "This unit is large and has four bedrooms. My thoughts were that Amanda and I remain here if that is agreeable with my lovely mate."

Amanda smirked. "I want to refrain from commenting until I hear the rest."

"Fair enough. The unit next door is almost as large and has three bedrooms."

Caroline cocked her head to the side. "You mean Mandy's apartment?"

"*Sì*, Caroline."

Amanda nodded. "I think I know where you're going with this. Go on."

"There is a secret door in the pantries that join the units, which would put Rafael close enough. If everyone is agreeable, I propose we move Rafael and Caroline into your old apartment, *tesoro*."

Amanda smiled. "That sounds like a good plan." She shrugged. "There is a small problem, though."

"Oh?"

"Yeah, you destroyed the place Thursday night.

Remember?"

Marco laughed softly. "*Sì*, protecting you. But, I am sure you will be surprised to know that as soon as you and the elders took off to go to Germany, the rest of the pack started working on restoring the damages. Clara assured me before our plane took off to come home that the unit would be complete, and your things would be transferred to this apartment before we arrived. Your things are here, so I am assuming that the repairs are completed as well."

"It sounds like you've been thinking about this," Amanda said.

"I started thinking on those lines when Caroline agreed to become Rafael's mate."

Amanda glanced at her friend. "Caroline, what do you think?"

Caroline looked at Rafael, and when he nodded, she smiled. "I'm in if Rafael agrees."

Rafael pulled Caroline over onto his lap and kissed her cheek. "*Sì, piccolo*, I think that would make things easier on us all." He then growled in her ear. "I am all for more privacy."

When Amanda smiled, Marco nodded. "Good. It seems like we are all in agreement. As soon as we have finished here, we can all go next door and inspect the repairs."

Amanda's eyes widened. "There's more?"

Marco blew out an extended breath. "*Sì*, I wish to make more changes at the advertising agency as well. Since I fired Charlie, I have decided to do some rearranging in management and clean house, so to speak."

Amanda and Caroline exchanged glances. "What kind of changes?" Caroline asked.

"When I bought the controlling share in Glasko Advertising, John and Margo expressed an interest in selling out totally. I declined at the time, but I think Amanda and I will take them up on their original offer."

Amanda blinked in confusion. "We will?"

"*Sì.* I figured that Amanda would take the position of vice president of the corporation, and she could handle the executive accounts. We could appoint Caroline as the office manager. I saw her leadership abilities when she stood up to Charlie in the lobby. I believe she will be well suited for the job."

"But that's Walter's job," Caroline protested.

"Walter has already put in a request for his retirement. Will you accept the promotion, Caroline?"

Smiling, Amanda nodded at her friend. "Go for it, baby girl."

A huge smile spread across Caroline's face. "Okay, I'll do it."

"Good. I have also decided to put Rafael into the position of head of security. As my enforcer, it will keep him informed of everything going on in the building, and in turn, he will report to me and keep me informed. Since Amanda has transcended, I am not anticipating any more trouble, but you never know."

Rafael placed Caroline on her feet and nodded as he stood up. "I like that idea. I can still perform my duties to you and keep an eye on my mate at the same time."

Marco stood. "Since I have no objections, I will call our attorneys and have the papers drawn up as soon as we have inspected the apartment." Amanda stood as well. "If all is satisfactory, you both can move your things as soon as you are ready."

CHAPTER TWENTY-ONE

Amanda and Caroline stepped off the service elevator into the parking garage. "I appreciate you and Marco helping us move," Caroline said.

"That's what friends are for, baby girl," Amanda said as she popped the hatch to Caroline's SUV. She handed Caroline two bags. "Take these two upstairs. I'll be right behind you."

Caroline paused. "Marco said I wasn't supposed to leave you by yourself."

"I'll be right behind you," she said as she nudged Caroline toward the elevator. "If we wait for each other, this'll take all day. Just go. Tell Marco I'll be right up."

"Okay," Caroline said, stepping inside the elevator. "It's your funeral."

Amanda rolled her eyes. "Funny, baby girl," she said as the doors closed. She turned back to the SUV and reached deep inside, tugging at a bag in the back. "Come here, you stupid—"

"Stupid what?" Amanda heard just before everything went black.

~*~

Amanda woke up on what felt like a hard floor to a constant seesaw rocking. The air was damp and rancid, smelling of mildew and rotting fish. The rocking, along with the smell, made her stomach lurch, and her mouth had the metallic taste of blood. She moaned; turning her head, she felt a sharp pain at the back of her skull, and when she tried to open her eyes, she was met with blackness.

She attempted to move her arm and discovered that she couldn't move. Her hands and feet were bound together by a rope. Amanda lay there, doing a mental assessment of her injuries. The only one she could detect was the knot on the back of her head. *Now what?* Ran through her mind.

Amanda?

Marco? She opened her eyes again, straining to see in the darkness. *Where are you?*

Looking for you.

Thank God.

What happened?

I don't know. The last thing I remember was trying to pull a bag out of the SUV, and everything went black.

Who took you?

I don't know.

Did you see anything?

No.

Did you smell or hear anything?

Amanda thought back. *Yes. I heard something.*

What?

I was fighting with the bag, trying to get it out of the back of the SUV. I was calling it stupid, and I distinctly heard someone say, 'stupid what?'

Did you recognize the voice?

No...I don't know.

Think hard.

Marco, my head hurts.

I'm sorry, tesoro, but this is important. For some reason, something is masking your smell. We can't seem to find you.

It might have been Charlie's voice, but I'm not sure. Why would he do this to me, Marco?

Revenge.

But I didn't do anything to him.

I did. I fired him.

Yeah, I remember that. Remind me to kick his ass the next time I see him.

There won't be a next time, tesoro. He won't live that long.

Give me a minute. I hear footsteps.

Tell me where you are. She heard the urgency in his voice.

I don't know.

A wedge of light flooded into the room as the door creaked open. Amanda closed her eyes to nearly shut, pretending to sleep.

"Stop pretending to be asleep, bitch. I heard you moan. I know that you're awake." Amanda opened her eyes and glared at Charlie. "Not so high and mighty now, are you bitch?"

"I don't know what you're talking about, Charlie. Now, let me go."

"Or what?"

"What do you mean by that?"

"What are you going to do if I don't? I mean, I have you trussed up like a Thanksgiving turkey. You ain't going anywhere unless I decide to let you go." He shook his head. "I don't see that happening." He laughed. "Even if you somehow managed to escape, you have nowhere to run. You're surrounded by water."

Where are you?

From the way he's ranting and the smell in this room, I'd have to say I'm on a fishing boat. "You'll go to prison for kidnapping, Charlie. Let me go, and I won't press charges."

Like Hell, you won't.

Marco, please, let me handle Charlie.

"They won't ever find your body."

"What?"

"I'm going to fuck you just to hear you scream, and I won't stop until I've had my fill of the high and mighty Amanda Archer."

I'm going to rip that mother fucker to shreds.

"That would be adding rape to the kidnapping charges, Charlie. Let me go. You're not using your head."

"Face it, bitch, you aren't going to live to see that precious boss of yours again. Fire me, will he? I'll show him that he just fucked with the wrong person."

Amanda, can you get loose from your bonds?

No, I don't think so.

Try to call your wolf forward. Just your hand. You need to break the ropes so that you can shift.

I haven't learned how to do that yet.

Crash course 101.

Oh, God.

Close your eyes and will her forward.

Amanda closed her eyes. *I'm trying.*

"Open your eyes, bitch!" Amanda's eyes flew open as she saw Charlie unzipping his pants. He pulled out his cock and fisted it. "First, I'm gonna jack off and cum all over you."

Try it now! Marco screamed in her head.

"Then, I'm gonna cut those clothes off of you and see how loud I can make you scream."

Amanda felt her claws extend on her right hand. *I think it's working.*

Good, now cut the ropes.

"What's wrong with your eyes, bitch?" he said as he jerked hard on his cock. "Those are some fucked up contacts. I need to find out where you got 'em before I kill you. They would be something added to my collection. I'll make the bitch I'm fucking at the time put them on in remembrance of you."

"You're sick, Charlie."

Her claws easily sliced the rope. *I'm free.*

Now kill him!

"Don't say that!" he yelled.

What? I can't. He's sick.

It is him or you.

I can't.

Your wolf will do what you cannot seem to do for yourself.

What?

As your alfa, I command you to shift.

Charlie kicked her in the side as her wolf burst forward. His body hurled through the air, slamming into the wall with her mighty jaws clamped on his neck. With a twist of her head, she snapped his neck and let his body crumple to a heap on the floor. Objects crashed to the floor around his body.

Her wolf was in a rage, destroying everything in her path.

He is dead. Calm down, l'amore.

Amanda crashed through the doorway, scrambling up the steps. She needed to run. She needed the stench of death out of her nostrils. Amanda sprang from the stairwell and skidded to a stop.

The boat rocked idly in the middle of the water. There wasn't another soul or boat in sight. There was nowhere to run. She sat down on her haunches and howled mournfully.

As your alfa, I command you to shift, Marco said softly.

Amanda sat huddled on the deck of the boat. The cool breeze blew her hair in her face and tickled her naked body.

I feel so ashamed. She wept.

Don't.

I can't help it.

Come home.

I can't. I don't know where I am.

Think of me and come home.

You mean teleport?

Sì.

Marco, I don't know how I did that.

Think of me. Can you do that for me?

Yes.

As your alfa, I command you home.

Amanda collapsed in his arms as the tears fell. Caroline placed a robe over her body as Marco hugged her to him and rocked her. "I have you now, *l'amore.* You are safe. You will be fine," he crooned softly.

Caroline and Rafael left their apartment through the

pantry, leaving them to their privacy.
~*~

Amanda sat cuddled in Marco's lap with the TV on. She was flipping through the channels randomly as he rocked her. She stopped on the news channel.

"Breaking news," the reporter said. "Local police have just found a boat floating in the middle of Lake Michigan. The scene inside the boat looks like a massacre. Although only one body has been located, there are women's clothes shredded, and everything inside the boat has been destroyed. The police suspect that foul play is involved but have no leads. The police have identified the body as the boat owner, Charlie Granger, from Chicago. According to reports, Mr. Granger was last seen being escorted out of the Glasko building downtown by security. No further information is available. And remember you heard it from me first, Jenson James. Tune back in at ten for further updates."

Amanda turned the TV off. "Great, we've made the headlines."

"In time, this will all be just a bad memory," Marco said softly.

"I can't sleep, Marco. The scene keeps replaying in my head over and over."

"He was beyond saving."

"Was he?" Amanda shook her head in frustration. "I'm not so sure of that."

"I am positive of that."

She blew out a long breath. "I just wish I could forget."

"Is that what you really want?"

Amanda sighed again. "Yes. It has stolen my joy in life."

Marco tenderly brushed the hair away from her eyes. "So be it," he said softly. "You will forget."

Amanda closed her eyes and fell into a deep sleep.

EPILOGUE

Dropping to her knees, Amanda held her abdomen, screaming out in pain. Her head was swimming, and her body was drenched in sweat. It was time, and she had never been more frightened in her life.

Marco entered the bathroom and scooped her up into his arms, then transferred her to the bed. "Calm your heart, *tesoro*. The pups are ready to make an appearance. Everything will be fine. Clara is on her way."

She gripped his hand as another pain ripped through her. "It doesn't feel fine," she panted. "I feel like I'm being ripped in two."

Smiling, he kissed the back of her hand and ran a cloth over her sweat-soaked forehead. "I can sense what is going on within you. Everything is as it should be. Both you and our pups will be fine."

There was a knock at the door as Amanda screamed out in pain again. "Come in, Clara."

Clara entered the room, shutting the door behind her. She smiled. "Thank you again, alfa, for allowing me to stay here this week. I have been looking forward to witnessing the birth of my great-grandchildren."

"Nonna," Amanda reached with her other hand for her grandmother. "It hurts."

"*Sì*, Alessandra, I know. A woman must endure the brunt of the pain." Clara pushed Marco aside. "Luckily for you, our labors are short." She turned her head, pointing to the dresser. "Alfa, ready the blankets. Your children are coming now," Clara barked her order.

Marco turned and rushed to do as he was told.

The corners of Amanda's mouth turned up in a pained smile. "I wouldn't have believed that if I hadn't seen it for myself. He doesn't take orders from anyone."

Clara laughed softly. "He is a proud one, but he has a good heart. He will make a good father."

Amanda nodded as another pain had her shoulders coming up off the bed.

"Alfa, support her shoulders. It is time."

Marco scooted past Clara and held his mate.

"Now, Alessandra, I need you to push with the next pain."

Amanda nodded and caught her breath, bearing down with the next pain.

"That is it, Alessandra. Good girl," Clara said as she took the screaming child and held him up for Marco. "Your son." Marco smiled proudly.

Amanda laughed and cried at the same time, leaning her head back against Marco. "He is beautiful," she said.

"That he is, *l'amore*," he said as he mopped her forehead again.

Clara finished cleaning the baby up, swaddled him

in a fresh blanket, and placed him close to Amanda. "He is beautiful, child, I am a proud grandmother, but your work here is not finished. His sister is ready, too."

Amanda nodded. "I'm ready to get this over with, too."

"Okay, Alessandra, whenever you are ready—"

Amanda screamed again as another pain racked her body.

"Push, Alessandra. Focus all your strength on pushing."

She nodded frantically as she caught her breath again and pushed.

"Very good." Clara worked on the crying baby and wrapped her in a clean blanket. She handed child one to Marco and the other to Amanda. "You two have done well."

Clara had just finished cleaning Amanda up when there was a knock at the door. Clara lifted the blanket up to cover Amanda's body and answered the door.

Caroline looked past Clara to see Amanda. "Can we come in?"

"You may," Clara said as she stepped aside.

Caroline waddled up to the bed and sat on the edge. "They're beautiful, Mandy."

"Congratulations, Alfa," Rafael said. "We would have arrived sooner, but my mate nearly could not squeeze through the passage in the kitchen."

Caroline's eyes saucered when everyone laughed. "Rafael!"

Clara slapped Rafael on the back. "I will remain here for a few more days. It looks like your mate is about ready."

Caroline put her hand on the base of her back. "In more ways than one," she said. She turned to her friend. "Mandy, have you picked out any names?"

"Yes," Amanda smiled as she glanced up at Marco. "I allowed him to name them."

Marco sputtered. "Allowed?"

Amanda threw back her head and laughed at her mate. "Tell her what you've named them, *Amante.*"

"Our son is Nico; it means 'victor of the people.'"

Rafael nodded. "A fitting name for our alfa's son."

"Our precious daughter is Anjelica, meaning 'angel.'"

"That is so sweet," Caroline said. "However, if she is anything like her mother, she'll be anything but an angel."

Amanda's eyes saucered. "Caroline!"

The room erupted with laughter.

Marco bent down and kissed the top of Amanda's head. "I hope she is exactly like her mother; then, she will be perfect."

Look for book 2 of the Cry Wolf Series, Giovanni.

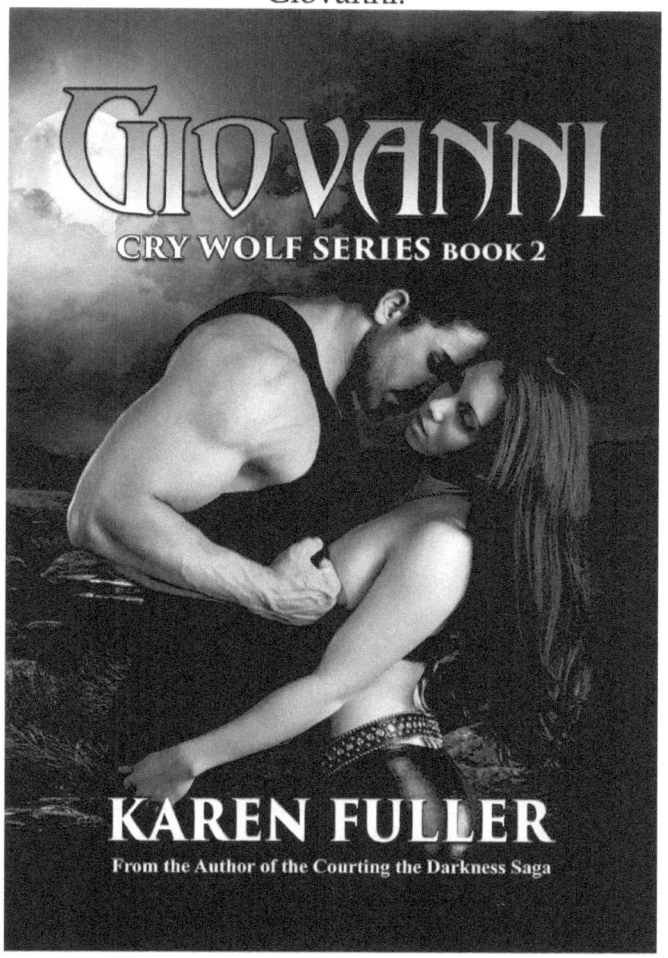

About the Author

Born in Northern Alabama, Karen Fuller learned to love the written word at the age of 12. She is a published author and writes Adult & Young Adult Paranormal Romance and Young Adult Historical Romance under her given name, and she writes children's middle-grade fiction under the pen name of K. G. Fuller. She also cowrites with Melissa Davis, Elissa Daye, and Erik Daniel Shein. She's an award-winning author and screenwriter and helps other authors further their careers. Please visit my websites. I am always adding something new. https://www.karenfullerauthor-screenwriter.com/ or http://www.worldcastlepublishing.com